PUZZLING M

Warren Clarke

Text copyright 2017

Warren Clarke

All Rights Reserved

Table of Contents

Chapter 1 1
Chapter 2 14
Chapter 3 27
Chapter 4 37
Chapter 5 47
Chapter 6 59
Chapter 7 71
Chapter 8 85
Chapter 9 98
Chapter 10 107
Chapter 11 118
Chapter 12 131
Chapter 13 143
Chapter 14 154
Chapter 15 166
Chapter 16 176
Chapter 17 189
Chapter 18 201
Chapter 19 216
Chapter 20 230
Chapter 21 241
Chapter 22 258
Chapter 23 267
Chapter 24 280
Chapter 25 290
Chapter 26 303

Chapter 27..315
Chapter 28..328

Chapter 1

The First Puzzle

Gregory Dawes, artist and lifelong misanthropist, slammed the car door shut, tucked his portfolio under his right arm, and strode towards the glass doors that marked the entrance to the building where these days he earned his living. Once upon a time he had worked in a national newspaper, with a daily cartoon to draw, under the caption 'Dawes Draws', but had been sacked for constantly attacking the political party of which his newspaper was a supporter. That wasn't the reason given to him. The editor had said he was repeating himself too much. He had felt insulted and offended by that; and if he hadn't already been an embittered man for no reason, the charge would have given him a good reason for being so. As it was, it didn't make much difference to his state of mind, and he soon found employment at Fothergill Puzzles at more or less the same salary.

It was his job to paint pictures that during the manufacturing process were cut up into tiles made of cardboard for purchasers of Fothergill jigsaws to fit together into a whole picture again. The harder they found that to do, the greater his satisfaction. The easier they found it, the less his sense of fulfilment. He had just finished his latest task, and was pleased with what he'd done. Ol' Fothergill was bound to like it. He wasn't the most demanding of employers at any time, but in this case the project was all his own, so maybe he would be a bit fussier than usual. Hard to see why, though. The clues couldn't be identified too easily, the colours were nicely balanced …

Gregory entered the building, nodded to Joan, the blond-haired receptionist, and made for the lift. He was a tall man, lean and stooping, with hunched shoulders, and was seldom seen without stubble on his chin and cheeks. His hair was greying and long, his eyes watery from peering closely at his work for extended periods; his cheeks were hollow and his nose hooked, with very often a bubble of snot emerging from it. And he always wore the same ragged, dirty blue jeans. In other words, one might have taken him for a down-and-out but for the portfolio, which marked him out as an artist of some kind and so justified his appearance, if not what was dribbling from his nostril.

The lift carried him to the second floor, where four offices, a staff toilet and a fire exit vied for his attention. He headed for the largest office – Ol' Fothergill's. Disdaining to knock, he walked straight in, nodded to Melissa, the blond-haired secretary, and asked: 'Is he in?'

Melissa, young and pretty – much prettier than Joan – knew her value as a secretary but overrated herself as a comedienne. She liked to think she always had a witty remark to make when men made advances or even when they didn't, and here was an ideal opportunity for her to demonstrate her drollery. Alas, and as usual, although a humorous rejoinder was there on the tip of her tongue, it stubbornly clung to it.

'Yes,' she replied instead, flashing her large blue eyes and smiling. She pressed a button on the intercom, lowered her head to within six inches of it, and said: 'Mr Fothergill – Mr Dawes is here.'

Gregory heard a voice sounding nothing like Mr Fothergill's tell the secretary to send him in.

'You can go in,' Melissa told him. So he nodded again as a kind of thank you, and went in.

A beaming Andrew Fothergill greeted him from behind his desk. Round-faced and rubicund, he was a large, round-bellied man who could only just fit into his chair without breaking the arms every time he sat down. As a lover of humanity, his attitude towards life was in such stark contrast to Gregory's that some kind of miracle seemed to occur at their every meeting, since they agreed so much over matters concerning the jigsaws that the company manufactured. The painting that Gregory now produced and laid on the table in front of his employer was a case in point. It proved to be exactly what Mr Fothergill had required.

'Yes, I can see it straight away,' he enthused, inspecting the work of art closely. 'The hand poking out from under the rug, the club in the fire, the dog's red feet…. I'm glad you didn't forget those; it shows that something very bloody has transpired.' He rubbed his hands together to convey his delight.

'But it won't be easy to decipher for everyone,' asserted Gregory defensively.

'Indeed not. I'm the one who suggested this particular murder, so I could hardly be expected not to figure out which murder was being depicted,' grinned Mr Fothergill, rubbing his hands together again to confirm his delight. 'And the murderer making his exit. I'm glad you haven't shown too much of him. That would have made it obvious which novel it is.'

'Well, it is a well-known novel, so maybe most people will get it anyway.'

Mr Fothergill shook his head. 'Don't you believe it. People don't read novels as much as they used to – not Victorian novels; although I guess some people will guess this one from seeing a film of it. There have been a few – famous ones too. Let's test it out, shall we? … Miss Morgan!' he cried. He wasn't one for modern technology, and refrained whenever possible from using even the intercom, which had been installed in his office fifteen years before. 'Miss Morgan!' he cried again, raising his voice (one gentle whisper in the intercom, of course, would have sufficed).

Nevertheless, Miss Morgan did respond, having pretty ears specially designed for picking up compliments made in low tones between young men. She entered the room with notepad and pencil, eager to be admired and pampered.

'Come closer, Miss Morgan, and look at this.'

On closer inspection, one could see that the secretary's cheeks were heavily powdered and hid how pretty her face was; that the pink mascara around her eyes distracted from how pretty her blue eyes were; and that the black beauty spot below one of her eyes concealed how pretty the skin was underneath. Overall, though, for all that, the effect on her face was one of outstanding prettiness, if not beauty.

'What is it?' she asked.

'It's our latest jigsaw – or it will be when the boys have turned it into one. Now, what do you see?'

Miss Morgan gazed down the painting, not entirely sure what she did see. She shook her head, reluctant to commit herself in case she said something foolish.

'I think you should explain what it is,' suggested Gregory.

'Yes, perhaps I should. What it is, Miss Morgan ... we have decided to make a series of jigsaws depicting famous murders – though without making it too clear which murder is *being* depicted. It will be up to the person putting the jigsaw together to guess which one. We're going to call the series – I've already decided on this,' Mr Fothergill said in an aside to Gregory. 'We're going to call it *Two Puzzles and One Murder*. What do you think of that, Mr Dawes? A good title?'

Gregory pursed his lips reflectively and nodded in a non-committal manner.

'One puzzle being the jigsaw, the second being the puzzle of which murder it is.' This explanation was for the benefit of Miss Morgan, who was still staring down at the painting. 'So ... the question for you, Miss Morgan, is which murder is being depicted in this painting. There are clues. You just have to identify them.'

Melissa frowned and then grimaced. 'Ooh, I don't know. I'm not very good at this sort of thing.'

'Think of a murder in a famous novel. Even if you haven't read the novel, I'm sure you'll have seen a film of it. There was even a musical made of it – a famous one. You must have seen that.' He paused a moment, then started singing. 'Fo-o-od, glorious food. Nothing quite like it for – Oh, no, I'm getting mixed up. Fo-o-od, glorious food …. Consider yourself our mate, consider yourself one of the family … You must know which musical those songs come from.'

Melissa seemed to think she knew, with the title on the tip of her tongue, but try as she might she couldn't quite –

'*Oliver*!' said Mr Fothergill.

'Oh, of course,'

'Well?'

'Well what?'

'Which murder is being depicted in the painting?'

Melissa gazed down at the painting again. 'Is it a murder?'

'Yes – that's what I'm saying. There are clues in the painting and you have to identify them and guess which it is…. A murder in *Oliver* … or actually a murder in *Oliver Twist*, since that's the title of the novel.'

'Oh, it's that woman, isn't it? What was her name?'

Mr Fothergill nodded encouragingly but in vain. He had to tell her.

'Nancy ... murdered by Bill Sikes. Clubbed to death. Look – you can see all the clues ... the club in the fire – Sikes burnt the weapon after the deed ... the dog's red feet – the red is the blood that the dog walked about in ...'

Melissa's expression became one of distaste. 'Ugh! I'm not sure I'd want to do a jigsaw like that.'

'You might not, but many would. People in the jigsawing fraternity are always looking for novelty, for something different, and this series of ours will, I'm sure, get them talking, discussing among themselves which murder they have puzzled together ... because we shan't tell them. We shall leave it an open question ... we'll never reveal the truth.'

Mr Fothergill sat back in his chair with his fingers interlocked over his tummy. But only for a second or two. Then he leaned forward and rubbed his hands together again.

'Go and get Mr Millar with an "a",' he told Melissa, watched her leave the room, then turned to Gregory. 'I'm rather pleased she didn't guess till I more or less told her. It shows that solving the mystery will require some thought.'

'Solving the mystery' seemed to Gregory a funny way of putting it, but he was as pleased as Mr Fothergill. He had been worried that if Melissa guessed correctly straight away, he'd be asked to make it more difficult. Once he'd made up his mind that a painting of his was finished, he had no liking for being told otherwise.

'I'm sure Mr Millar and the other men will be as excited as I am when I tell them about this new series of ours,' said Mr Fothergill. 'I've kept it between ourselves till now. I do hope you did likewise, as I asked, Mr Dawes.'

'I did,' confirmed the other. He wasn't in the business of mixing socially, and certainly not with anyone who spent his time doing jigsaws or cared two hoots about business plans regarding them. So he didn't find it difficult to remain silent about his involvement with them. He would have found it more difficult to admit to it. His ambition as an artist knew no bounds, and was focused primarily on having an exhibition of his 'unusual nudes', of which Mr Fothergill knew nothing. Gregory hadn't painted those to be turned into jigsaws.

Mr Millar soon arrived with Melissa in tow. He wore a knee-length white coat, was lean and narrow-shouldered, had short greasy hair in a right parting, and maintained a sober expression at the best and worst of times. This was neither, but the sober expression was obviously waiting for one or the other to return.

'Come and take a look, Mr Millar,' Mr Fothergill urged.

'You'll never guess what it is,' said Melissa. 'I didn't – not when I first looked at it, anyway.'

Mr Millar moved closer, placed his hands in the square pockets of his coat and inclined his head towards the table in a contemplative manner. As he pored over the painting, he fiddled in one pocket with a few coins and in the other with a bunch of keys. He wasn't aware of doing either.

He was a taciturn man, Mr Millar, a cause of enormous frustration to those who had dealings with him. Eliciting even a word, let alone an opinion, from him was a long slog. Mr Fothergill, well acquainted with his employee's 'foible', as he regarded it, wasn't about to be kept waiting on this occasion.

'Well … what d'you think?'

'I think you should explain what it is,' remarked Mr Dawes for the second time in his life.

So, not without some degree of impatience, Mr Fothergill did, ending with the inevitable question: 'So which murder do you think it is?'

'You'll never guess,' insisted Melissa. 'I didn't.' Her repeated admission was actually a plea for some kind of sympathy from one or other of the gentlemen present, but all three were much too engrossed in the painting to oblige.

Mr Millar's sober face hadn't budged from its set position.

'The clues are all there,' said Mr Fothergill.

'You won't know what they are just from looking,' laughed Melissa. 'I had to be told.'

'From a famous work of fiction,' Mr Fothergill prompted.

'Don't read much fiction,' declared Mr Millar, taking out his right hand from his pocket and starting to measure the painting with his thumb and forefinger. He wanted a rough estimate on how many average-size tiles would be needed to make up the jigsaw. Being the head of the manufacturing process, he was already thinking ahead.

Mr Fothergill could wait no longer. He told him which murder it was.

'See the dog with red feet, the club in the fire …'

'He'd never have got that,' insisted Melissa. 'I didn't.'

Mr Millar nodded sagely, though whether in agreement with Melissa or because he had figured out the exact number of tiles required was impossible to say, because, unlike the painting, he didn't provide any clues.

'Miss Morgan – go and get Mr Miller with an "e", Mr Grounds and Miss Thorson. We might as well tell the others about our latest project.'

Saying the words 'our latest project' seemed to confirm its existence, and pleased Mr Fothergill no end. It wouldn't be the last time he used them in the weeks and months to come.

Chapter 2

Further Suggestions

While waiting for the others to arrive, Mr Fothergill and Mr Millar entered into a more technical discussion regarding the best size of jigsaw for the painting. This very much depended on the painting's content – on how small or large the objects depicted were. Tiles that were too small could very often render the jigsaw more difficult than was good for future sales of other jigsaws, in that they tired out and ultimately bored the person trying to put it together. However much people liked doing jigsaws, there was a limit to their patience: even they had other things to do with their lives.

Mr Miller with an 'e' and Mr Grounds came in together without Melissa or Miss Thorson. Mr Miller was the company's financial expert. He worked out the manufacturing costs of their products and recommended the wholesale prices that would ensure a profit. He had thick lips, a bad breath smell, hairs protruding from his nose, had a nervous habit of constantly clearing his throat, usually wore the same dark pinstripe suit with matching waistcoat and tie, was serious of demeanour though not without a sense of humour, was efficient without being exciting, and was reliable ... though it has to be said that he had a darker side to his character of which no one at Fothergill Puzzles was aware: he attended séances. The idiot attended séances.

Mr Grounds was the company's sales representative. He did much of his work over the phone, but occasionally went out to retailers to twist their arms metaphorically. He was a younger man than the others – thirty at most; and as a direct result of his daily use of verbal persuasion to negotiate deals, he had a confident bearing and a slightly contemptuous attitude towards anyone resisting his advances ... Melissa included, despite the numerous ones he'd made. She had spurned them all. For as much as she was attracted to any good-looking man in trousers – and Mr Grounds wasn't bad-looking – she couldn't abide any man – good-looking or not – who wore a toupee. Mr Grounds wore a rather obvious one. Melissa hadn't revealed the reason for her rejection of him – she didn't want to hurt his feelings – and so he was doomed to receive the same negative response for as long as he persisted in his leering innuendoes and smutty remarks about her short skirts (both of which, too, may have had something to do with her rebuffs, acceptable though they might have been from Richard Gere, the love of her cinematic life).

'Gather round,' said the ebullient Mr Fothergill, waving them closer. 'See what you can see in this. We'll wait for Miss Thorson before I explain; she'll be here shortly.'

Miss Thorson's office was one floor above, a convenient location for any woman wishing to keep other people waiting for her grand appearance. Consequently, it was a very convenient location for Miss Thorson, who wasn't averse to making a grand appearance whenever the opportunity arose. So she didn't hurry down. Indeed, she didn't. She and Melissa had a little chat about women's things before, eventually, Melissa said they'd better get going and Miss Thorson reluctantly – if one were to judge by the speed at which she moved – agreed.

Blond-haired and wearing a tailor-made, fawn two-piece, she wasn't as pretty as Melissa but was prettier than Joan. She specialised in wry expressions with cocked eyebrows and was generally suspicious of any man who looked at her, which seemed to seem to her to be the preliminary move in an abusive relationship.

Her grand appearance was welcomed with the acclaim she thrived on by Mr Fothergill, if not by anyone else, since she wasn't the most popular employee at the company.

'Come and see, Miss Thorson,' said Mr Fothergill, who had no doubt she would recognise the murder scene at first glance. She was head of advertising, wrote the leaflets provided with the jigsaws, and so was obviously – it seemed to him – of a literary bent. She was bound to know *Oliver Twist*, so how could she not identify the brutal and bloody murder of poor Nancy?

But no ... she didn't. Melissa had been perfectly right when she told her on the way down that she'd never guess what it was. And she didn't.

'... so what we want from you, Miss Thorson,' said Mr Fothergill, after explaining again about the company's latest project, 'is to compose your leaflet in such a way that the mystery is not revealed ... and no extra clues are given. The only clues there should be are those in the jigsaw. What do you think, everyone – are we on to a winner, or are we on to a winner?'

There were murmurs of agreement from around the table. The truth was that nobody thought it a bad idea. And it was different from using photographs of famous paintings or familiar landscapes. Since Mr Dawes had joined the company, he had been asked to paint imaginary scenes with a humorous side to them, and it was a source of wonder to the other employees that someone so devoid of pleasantry and warmth managed to do it. But this latest project seemed more suitable: he would, they felt sure, do some good work on it.

And it was to be a long-running series, Mr Fothergill stressed.

'So we'll need suggestions on what other murders we can use. We might as well discuss that now, since you're all here; Mr Dawes will want one to work on when he leaves here.... Any ideas? ... Speak up,' he jollied them. 'Don't be shy.' He looked at everyone in turn, almost daring them to remain silent.

Mr Grounds was always quick in such situations; he liked to think he had a quick mind.

'The Kennedy assassination.'

Mr Fothergill waved a hand dismissively. 'No, no, no. That was a real-life murder. We're only interested in fictional murders.'

Mr Grounds couldn't possibly accept so immediate a rejection of his suggestion, so he persevered.

'It's probably the most famous murder in the history of the world ... unless Julius Caesar's is.'

'Yes, but we want only fictional murders, and President Kennedy was assassinated in real life, I think you'll find. It would be in extremely bad taste to exploit the murder of any real-life victim for purposes of profit. Fiction only, gentlemen ... and ladies.'

That slowed everything down. For some strange reason the only fictional murder that anyone immediately thought of was Bill Sikes' murder of Nancy, as though that would have been the first one they thought of if it hadn't already been used.

'Do films count?' asked Melissa.

Mr Fothergill hesitated. He really wanted a series of murders in novels, having little interest himself in films. 'Better if they were novels first, like *Oliver Twist*. In a way, I want these jigsaws to be educational and encourage reading. I like to think that somebody making the jigsaw and discovering that the murder depicted is from a novel he hasn't read will immediately go out and buy a copy' – a remark which for some reason made him chuckle.

Again there was prolonged silence as those present cast their minds back into their literary past to any novels they'd read in which a murder occurred. But there weren't many novels to choose from, as none of them had much interest in fiction.

'Come, Miss Thorson,' Mr Fothergill urged her, 'you must have read some novel that scared the living daylights out of you because of a murder described in it.'

Miss Thorson didn't appreciate being accused of taking fright at some silly novel; her reading was mainly of fashion and its history. Of that she was knowledgeable: of bloody melodrama she wasn't.

So now there was another prolonged silence while everyone waited for her to respond – which she didn't. She couldn't understand why, suddenly, it was *her* responsibility to reel out a list of titles. These jigsaws were Fothergill's idea in the first place, so why couldn't he come up with something else? He'd had longer to think about it than anyone else. It was outrageous really that –

Mr Miller with an 'e' interrupted her mental tirade.

'Othello's murder of Desdemona.'

Another dark secret of Mr Miller's: he knew some Shakespeare. As did Mr Grounds, actually, but he, having had his suggestion rejected, was in no mood to allow anyone else to avoid the same fate.

'That's a play, *Othello* – not a novel.'

It *was* a play, not a novel: but it was – *literature.* And that was the important thing for Mr Fothergill. He took ten seconds to digest the suggestion and then clasped his hands together in a gesture of triumph.

'Yes – that's a good idea. Thank you, Mr Miller. Othello murdering Desdemona. I remember seeing the play in my student days. There was a handkerchief involved, wasn't there? You could use that, Mr Dawes, as one of the clues.'

Mr Dawes had been quiet for a while. But he now pointed out that he didn't know the play at all.

'Then borrow a copy from the local library – or buy one, of course. It shouldn't take you long to sort out some other clues. Excellent – that's a start. Any other suggestions? ... Wait. I have one myself: *The Murder of Roger Ackroyd*. Agatha Christie's first novel, wasn't it? A famous country-house murder. Yes, we'll do that as well. You've got some reading ahead of you, Mr Dawes. I take it you don't know the *Roger Ackroyd*?'

Gregory shook his head.

'Then get a copy. Expenses on the company, of course, if necessary.... Good. Well, we'll leave at that for the moment; Mr Dawes can't paint too many pictures at once. But do let me emphasise one thing. This is very hush-hush. Reveal to no one what our plans are. You may not think that anyone you know is involved in jigsaws, as you yourself are, but you can't be sure that even if they aren't they won't reveal them to someone who is. Secrecy is important in all kinds of business enterprises, but especially, I believe, in that of jigsaws. We have the chance to corner the market in this particular area. Let's not shoot ourselves in the foot.'

It was like a call to arms. Or like Noel Coward's rousing captain's speech to his men in the film *In Which We Serve*. And there, if Mr Fothergill had been cinematically inclined, was an idea for another series of jigsaws: *Two Puzzles and One Film*. Mr Dawes could have painted a picture portraying a film whose title could be worked out only by identifying the clues provided. Exactly the same sort of thing as with *Two Puzzles and One Murder*. But Mr Fothergill was more a lover of Charles Dickens than of David Lean, much as he'd enjoyed the latter's film version of the very novel chosen for the first murder puzzle.

And it was a good first choice, Mr Fothergill thought, congratulating himself later. He had decided on it without any assistance, had set the wheels in motion without any encouragement, and soon, thanks to him and his team (credit where it was due), the resulting jigsaw would be available in shops around the country for the enjoyment of all.

Mr Miller too congratulated himself as he squeezed into the driver's seat of his car after finishing work for the day. He loosened his tie almost as a prize to himself for being the person who had suggested Othello's murder of Desdemona. No one else had. They'd been stuck for ideas until he spoke up. It was funny, he thought, how inspiration seizes one. It was some time since he'd watched a play by Shakespeare, yet all of a sudden there it was – the flash of inspiration. And it wasn't that he was used to racking his brains for inspiration: he was an accountant, after all, who couldn't let his imagination run away with him. Where would the company be if he did? How financially secure? Yet when called upon he had been equal to the challenge. Strange, really. He didn't even like the play. That blackie strangling that poor girl. It was disgusting, showing that on the stage....

What was disgusting in the opinion of the simmering Chester Grounds was the rejection of his – yes, *his* – Kennedy assassination as the next murder puzzle. As he drove home he fulminated to himself about how silly it was to concentrate on fictional murders. Most people know more about real-life murders than they do about fictional ones. Only those who read Charles Dickens would have any chance of guessing the murder depicted in that puzzle. But who didn't know about the Kennedy assassination? Even people who weren't born at the time knew about it. The clues would have been easy to include in the painting: a pile of books suggesting the Book Depository, an open-topped car, a stars-and-stripes, say.... Then they could have followed that with ... what? ... Dr Crippen's murder of his wife … Jack the Ripper's – well, no, that would be too extreme for a puzzle. But hell's bells, thought Chester, there were plenty of murders that weren't as gruesome as his. No – ol' fatty had spoken: fictional murders it had to be.

Melissa lived only a short distance away and so walked home. She was pleased that no one else had guessed what the murder was. It was silly, really, to try to find clues in a painting when one didn't know what the painting was about. Once she'd known it was based on *Oliver* – the film, that is – she had no problem identifying the murder even without the clues. No one else had done that – not even Alysse….

Alysse Thorson drove home in her Peugeot, hating every second of her time behind the wheel. There was far too much traffic for her liking. There always was. She often felt shrieking at other drivers for being in front of her and slowing her down, or indeed for being behind her when she thought they were too close, or for causing her to stop when the traffic lights allowed them to go. Hardly a journey went by when she didn't see herself sitting in the back and being chauffeured. That was something she had ambitions towards. Hardly a day at the office went by when she didn't see herself as Mr Fothergill's partner or as someone so crucial to the running of the company that she was involved in every decision and was always so busy that she needed the aforesaid chauffeur to drive her about – though she couldn't have said to where exactly – while she carried on with her work.

Mr Millar with an 'a' stayed late in his office to start on the plans for the jigsaw's manufacture, his resolutely sober expression belying any enthusiasm he may have been feeling for it; while Mr Dawes, leaving before anyone, called in not at the library but at a convenient public house, where he would stay till a resolutely sober expression on *his* features became impossible to imagine.

Chapter 3
The First Big Test

It was a habit of Mr Fothergill's to allow his wife Vera the privilege of testing every jigsaw the company made. Unless it received his wife's seal of approval, he liked to say half-jokingly to his employees, they couldn't go ahead with marketing the product. If his wife got no pleasure from it, he insisted, they couldn't expect anyone else to. It wasn't usually a problem: Mrs Fothergill enjoyed doing jigsaws, whatever the theme or content, be they of landscapes, flower arrangements or cute little kittens. So once *Two Puzzles and One Murder No. 1* was all but ready for the shops, Mr Fothergill took the jigsaw home and solemnly presented it to his wife 'for immediate consideration'.

In the past such a heartfelt appeal had caused Mrs Fothergill to miss an episode of *Coronation Street*, her favourite television programme. And it did again on this occasion. Mrs Fothergill knew how much Andy – she was the only person in the world to call him that – valued her opinion, and she couldn't wait to get started, rushing the dishes after dinner so she could toss the tiles onto the dining table and finish the jigsaw, hopefully, before bedtime.

In her sixties now, her once blond hair was a dyed white hiding the grey streaks; but in her younger days she had been almost as pretty as Melissa and much prettier than Joan, though it would have been a matter of some debate whether she was prettier than Alysse. Mr Fothergill would have thought she was – of course he would – and indeed wouldn't have heard a bad word about her in any respect. Theirs had been a very happy marriage, boasting at the latest count two children and four grandchildren, all of whom enjoyed doing jigsaws – if none more than Mrs Fothergill, as could be seen by the intense concentration she gave to the pieces on the table in front of her.

Every now and then Mr Fothergill glanced across from behind his newspaper – he wasn't one for watching television – to gauge how well she was progressing. But for a long while he said nothing, not wanting to distract his wife from her task and silently admiring the skill with which she successfully joined two tiles together.

She wore tiny square spectacles, Mrs Fothergill, to help her focus on objects close to hand. When Mr Fothergill finally asked her how she was doing, she turned her head and peered over the top of her spectacles towards him; they were useless for anything more than two feet away.

'Don't rush me, dear,' she remonstrated half-jokingly; for just as at times Mr Fothergill liked to say things in a half-jocular manner, so did she. Who had picked up the habit from the other was impossible to say, though no doubt one of them had led the way.

'I was thinking of *Coronation Street*, Vera. I wouldn't want you to miss that.'

'I've been watching *Coronation Street* for fifty years. I can miss one episode while I'm doing this.'

Mr Fothergill smiled. She was so supportive. And he had no doubt that once she had completed the jigsaw, she would immediately recognise the murder depicted; she was just as much an avid reader of Dickens as he was. He recalled with a broader smile the tug-of-war between them for a copy of *Martin Chuzzlewit*, which at that time neither had read. They had solved the problem by passing the book back and forth between themselves so that, first, one could read a chapter, and then the other could. It worked quite well; they had a lot of fun discussing the events in the narrative as they moved towards the novel's climax, disagreeing over which characters were the best and whether certain twists in the plot were a mark of the author's genius or his self-indulgence. That was the fun. Happy marriages were as much about how couples coped with disagreements as they were about living in complete harmony at all times. Younger people, they liked to say, didn't seem to understand that.

It was two hours before Mrs Fothergill sat back in triumph, gazing down at the completed jigsaw. Mr Fothergill got up and went over to her, peering over her shoulder at the picture.

'Now then,' he said, 'any idea which murder it is?'

Mrs Fothergill leaned forward, inspecting every part of the painted scene.

To have worked it out immediately would not have been exactly what Mr Fothergill was hoping for, and Mrs Fothergill realised this, so it wasn't surprising that she hummed and hahed, and wondered about this and queried that, and frowned and wrinkled her nose in what had been one of the most seductive of her habits when she and Mr Fothergill started courting and indeed was the very feature that had first attracted him to her.

But she couldn't guess what the murder was.

Or if she could, she preferred to pretend she couldn't – for Mr Fothergill's sake, as she perceived it … whether it made sense or not.

So when she gave up and claimed she had no idea, Mr Fothergill was understandably perplexed.

'Look at the dog,' he urged. 'See how red its legs are. What does that tell you? See all the red on the floor. What d'you think that is?'

'Well, blood, I assume, seeing as it's a murder scene.'

'That's right. So which murder took place with a dog as a witness, walking about in the blood as he watched the murderer bludgeon his victim to death? You've read the novel, so you should know.'

'My memory's going these days. I'm not getting any younger, dear.'

'Nonsense. You always remember birthdays. I never do.' He broke into song. 'Fo-o-o-d, glorious food ... Consider yourself our mate, consider yourself part of –'

'Oh, *Oliver*, of course.... Bill Sikes murdering Nancy.'

'That's right, but let's have the proper title, dear – *Oliver Twist*. That's the title of the novel. The jigsaw's showing us a *fictional* murder – one inside a novel. No prize if you give us the title of a film based on it.'

'Prize – is there a prize?'

'No; that's just my way of talking ... unless the prize is simply the satisfaction one feels at solving the mystery.'

'Mystery?'

'The mystery of which murder is being depicted.'

'Ah! Well, I did solve it, and I have to say I feel a great satisfaction.'

Mr Fothergill coughed with that tact which is slightly apologetic in indicating a slight objection to what is being claimed.

'With a little more help than perhaps you should have had,' he remarked. 'You were at a loss till my deep baritone rang out. I would hate to think that everyone doing the jigsaw would need a few songs to help them. Why –' Mr Fothergill fell silent and remained so for a few seconds. 'Now, there's an idea, Vera: singing jigsaws. Jigsaws that as one puts them together, the pieces sing in some way. What d'you think? A good idea? I'll have to mention that to Mr Millar and the others. Hear what they have to say. Hmm … it could work, especially if we do jigsaws of famous musicals … like *Oliver* or … *Oklahoma*. That's one you like isn't it?'

But Mrs Fothergill was already putting away the pieces of *Two Puzzles and One Murder No. 1*, and was apparently too busy to answer.

The following morning, Mr Fothergill had forgotten all about the singing jigsaws. Once he arrived at his office, he had a new design for the box of *Two Puzzles and One Murder No. 1* to consider. Normally, of course, the box of any jigsaw showed the picture to be constructed from the tiles inside. That wouldn't do for a jigsaw that had to be explored for clues to a murder; the people thinking of buying it would have been able to identify the murder simply by seeing the outside of the box in the shop. So something else was needed. Mr Dawes had been working on it for some time, and had finally come up with the picture of a magnifying glass surrounded by loose tiles, while underneath the glass was a tile of enhanced size (because of the magnification) in which 'No. 1' was written. Mr Fothergill was delighted with it, and couldn't praise Mr Dawes enough.

'It's very striking,' he declared; 'and that's terribly important. It's so easy for any jigsaw to be swallowed up by the vast array of other jigsaws on sale. We need ours to stick out from all the rest, and, by George, Mr Dawes, I think you've hit on the very thing. I love that magnifying glass.'

So that was the box in which *Two Puzzles and One Murder No. 1* was delivered to retail shops around the country to vie with the products of the company's competitors.

And successfully vie it did. Sales from day one were exceptional. Miss Thorson's description on the back of the box certainly played its part in encouraging people to buy. Without in any way hinting at which murder could be found inside, she enticed and intrigued them with a blurb that would have done a writer of thrillers proud.

'I always thought you had a literary bent,' Mr Fothergill had told her on first reading it. And even Alysse had flushed at the praise, while at the same time resenting it. She hated it when men patronised her, or even when they didn't but were obviously thinking of doing so. It was none of their business whether she had a literary bent or not!

But the jigsaw's success couldn't be denied, and she had every reason to feel pleased with herself, especially as not everyone who bought it after reading her blurb was used to buying jigsaws. Indeed, parents who regularly bought them for their children hesitated over purchasing one with the title *Two Puzzles and One Murder*. The word 'murder' was the problem. Anything to do with murder was hardly suitable for younger children in particular. Not that their reluctance mattered; it was more than made up for by the number of people who bought the jigsaw *because* of the word 'murder'. They didn't buy it for their children: they bought it for themselves. They were those who read novels and true stories *about* murder, and watched films about murder; those whose lives were seemingly enhanced by an *obsession* with murder.

One such person was Edgar Rice Root, whose father had been a fan of the *Tarzan* stories. He had called in at the local Smith's for a car magazine, and this particular word 'murder' on a box of jigsaws caught his attention. As casually as he could, he drifted over and picked up the box for a closer look. He read the blurb with a smile, then a chuckle, and then took the jigsaw over to the counter, paying for it in cash. He couldn't remember ever having done a jigsaw in his life. But he was keen to do this one, even though he wasn't a reader of fiction and didn't expect to guess the murder depicted.

But he was a murderer, which kind of explains his interest.

Chapter 4

The First Murder

His father was his first victim. He had pushed him in his wheelchair over some cliffs on Blackpool's north shore. He was only twelve at the time, and his tearfully feigned distress at having 'lost control' as he slowly manoeuvred the wheelchair down the winding path was convincing enough to stifle any suspicion on the part of the police of a deliberate act – though even the tears weren't necessary: twelve-year-old boys didn't do that sort of thing to their fathers. Who could believe that they would?

This one did. And it wasn't that he hated his father, or that he resented having to do so much for him due to his diabetes. They'd had good times together. But if a man – or a twelve-year-old boy –

has the devil in him, so to speak, friendship or familial ties count for nothing when the urge comes on him, as it did that morning, when serious injury was the least his father could have expected as he toppled over the edge.

He wouldn't have expected that after the funeral his son would burn all his Tarzan memorabilia. There were some collectors' items among the comics, and it would have broken his heart to see them end up as ashes. But Edgar did it with his mother's approval. She had always been embarrassed by her husband's curious predilection, and had often mocked him with her friends. Edgar had heard her do it and hated her for it, even though he had mocked him with his own friends – the one or two he had at school. He had never taken to the Tarzan stories himself. His father had read them to him when he was little, but he felt no sense of identification with a man who lived in the jungle, swung from tree to tree, was muscular and had no fear of wild animals. *He* didn't live in a jungle, loathed sports, was flabby, and was scared to death of the Alsatian next door. So he and his mother burnt the lot, he spitefully, she with relief. And if she had done it spitefully he would have done it with relief, or with some other emotion – anything as long as it was different from his mother's. For Edgar had even less affection for his mother than he'd had for his father, and if her dead body wouldn't have seemed too suspicious immediately after the death of his father, he might have quickly found a way of murdering her as well. As it was, he thought it better to wait a few years. She was a good cook and he liked her food, so he might as well have the benefit ... at least till he was twenty. He should have figured out another perfect crime by then.

He didn't have to. His mother died of cancer when he was eighteen. He inherited the house, made a career in selling insurance, and decided his next perfect crime would have to be perpetrated on somebody else.

He bided his time for several years. But eventually the opportunity arose in Poulton-le-Fylde. He had clients there, and had been asked by one to call at a neighbour's a few doors away. She was an elderly woman by the name of Edith Shepherd who had been persuaded to take out insurance on her life and various other things, something she had never done before. Edgar had acquired a reputation for being honest and fair – which he was when it suited his purpose – and so her friend hadn't hesitated to recommend him.

When he made his first call on her he probably had no intention of killing her; his only thought was for his commission on what he would manage to extract from her honestly and fairly. It was only when the silly woman confided that her distrust of bankers had led her to keep a large portion of her savings at home that his wish to commit another murder resurfaced – which it did almost at once.

'I hope you don't keep it under the mattress,' he had joked.

Oh no, she didn't do that.

Then ten minutes later:

'Whatever you do, don't keep it in a drawer. Burglars always look in drawers.'

No, she didn't keep it there either.

She didn't reveal exactly where she kept it, but it wasn't under the mattress and it wasn't in a drawer; Edgar didn't press the matter beyond that for fear of arousing suspicion.

He was very patient. He sold her some insurance (honestly and fairly) and then left her alone for a few months. When he visited her again he did so without a preliminary telephone call to let her know he was coming. And he went at night, when it was dark. He parked a few streets away, checked that there was no CCTV in the avenue where she lived, made sure that no one else was about, then slipped through the front gate and rang the doorbell, hoping against hope that she didn't have any other visitors. But she lived alone and he knew she had only one offspring: a daughter who lived in Australia. So unless the daughter had come home to see her mother …

She hadn't. Mrs Shepherd had no other visitors that night. Nor any visitors ever again. For Mrs Shepherd was strangled that night, after she had revealed where her money was. Strangled with Edgar's scarf to the accompaniment of the strange gurgling sounds she made. He hadn't wanted any blood to get spattered on his clothes, and he was obviously strong enough to despatch a little old woman, so the scarf had seemed the ideal weapon, as it proved to be. Then, surreptitiously, he left the house.

The murder had never been solved. Nor had any of his subsequent murders. Four in all over several years. Three silly old women and one silly old man, only two of whom had taken out insurance with him. He wasn't foolish enough to allow the police to spot a link like that; they would have been on to him in no time. As it was, no one from the police had ever come to question him. He was free to murder again whenever the temptation or desire overtook him.

Or was it a compulsion? For there was a link between the murders, albeit a deliberately created one by Edgar himself: a full moon. He had learnt that quite by chance his murder of Mrs Shepherd had been carried out on one such night. It occurred to him that if – when – he murdered again, it would be as well to do it on a similar night. It would give the police the impression that they were looking for a lunatic of some sort and not for someone as clever as he was. The idea merely amused him at first but came to be something that was very much a part of his murder plan when the urge came. He would prepare everything well in advance and – as long as nothing cropped up to thwart him – commit the crime as the full moon shone in the sky (or would have done but for the clouds). It had worked out very nicely; nothing *had* thwarted him, and his tally of successful murders continued to grow.

Edgar struggled with the jigsaw for three hours on and off. He frowned and got frustrated, and if there hadn't been the picture of a murder to keep his interest he would have probably dumped the pieces in the bin. He muttered and swore and cursed the manufacturers, and for a time wondered whether he'd ever finish the damn thing.

But of course he did, and then he gazed down at the picture, puzzling over what it portrayed. He felt that as a murderer himself he should know. Yet the blood – the red was obviously blood – on the dog's legs meant nothing to him. He had the sense to realise that that was one of the clues, but at first it was the only one he could identify. He wasn't sure whether anything else was. He checked on the box. Yes, the word 'clues' was plural. There had to be others. He carefully inspected every square inch with his eyes. That thing in the fire – that could be one. What the hell was it? A club, by the looks of it. Yes – the murder weapon, of course. So that *was* a clue.

A clue, yes, but one that meant no more to him than the dog's bloody legs. He couldn't figure it out. When he went to bed that night he was still wondering what it could be, even though he knew he had no chance of guessing. It preyed on his mind because of the humiliation he felt. As a professional, he felt it was something he should know. So he cursed the manufacturers again as he tried his best to fall asleep.

And he did again the following morning as he shaved in front of the bathroom mirror. He had soft, sensitive skin and used an electric razor which left a faint morning shadow on his cheeks and chin. He hated cutting himself, which he used to do regularly with a non-electric one; but the shadow gave him a slightly sinister look, which, all things considered, was a bit of a handicap. He stared at his reflection: his wide fleshy jaw, the narrow eyes suggesting he wanted to watch other people from behind the cover of his eyelids, the nose with its habitually flaring nostrils, the dark wavy hair…. Nothing particularly attractive, it has to be said. A psychologist might have assumed that his murderous activities had their root in the inadequacy he felt at not being handsome. But no. Nothing so trite … though it might have been a clue to his own murders if a jigsaw had been made of them. Something ugly in the picture. No, that wouldn't work. Who would know the murderer was ugly, if it wasn't known who the murderer was?

He smiled and looked at the reflection of the electric razor in his hand, waving slightly as if to draw attention to it.

Now there was a clue: the razor.

Or better: the discarded one in the bin.

He chuckled. Who the hell would guess his identity from seeing that in a jigsaw?

He had left the jigsaw intact on the kitchen table, so as he munched his morning toast and drank his coffee his eyes roamed over the picture once again. The dog's bloody legs, the club in the fire ... And it wasn't long before his mind started wandering. It occurred to him that if he'd battered one of his victims with a club and taken a dog with him so that its legs got bloody, that picture, that jigsaw, would have depicted one of his own murders. It was a pity he hadn't. He liked the idea of a jigsaw – of jigsaws – commemorating his crimes. Even if no one ever knew that he, Edgar Root, was the killer, it would be one way of going down in history, though no doubt a book would be written about them some day. He was disappointed that none had appeared so far; he would have liked to read it. But a jigsaw had a peculiar appeal. Children do jigsaws, and the image he conjured up of a young child, with his tongue out in concentration, trying to figure out the murder depicted, was one he cherished.

Coffee drunk, toast finished, he went off to work, which, when he wasn't travelling about, he started at nine and finished at five. He was a regular sort of guy in that respect. And he wasn't unpopular. None of his colleagues was close to him, but he often joined a few of them in the nearest pub for a drink at lunchtime. He had a dry sense of humour which they particularly appreciated. He never drank too much or lost his temper in front of anyone. To do so would have been dangerous for someone like him; he had secrets to preserve, and drunkenness or a bad temper could let them out however tight-lipped he tried to be.

So nobody for a second suspected him of having committed murders. Everyone would have been amazed at the revelation.

Just as they would have been on learning that he'd started doing jigsaws.

Chapter 5

More About Killing

The curious thing about Edgar is that when he was little he'd never tortured or killed animals. Lots of children do – and that was the point, as far as Edgar was concerned. It was kids' stuff. He had watched once as two other boys applied a lit match to a cat's tail to see what effect on the cat it had, but he'd wandered away before they subjected the creature to anything worse (not that he'd tried to stop them, of course).

So one would have to conclude that he wasn't at heart a sadistic person. Nor did he obtain any sexual gratification from his murders. No orgasm for him as he strangled an elderly member of the opposite sex. He obviously got some satisfaction from his wicked deeds, but it was more a sense of achievement, of a job well done. Very little more, in fact, than what he felt after selling a particularly expensive form of insurance. A little more, but only a little. He was actually a very conscientious employee of Gillard & Sons, the company where he worked. But yes, a little more.

For one thing, he had to do all the preparation himself. There was nothing already written down in the form of a contract. All the lies, in other words, were his to invent. And *he* took the risk – nobody else. He – nobody else – faced imprisonment if captured and found guilty, which he probably would be because he had no intention of ever pleading innocent. He'd thought about that a lot. There wouldn't be any point. If the police ever brought him to trial, it would be because they had the evidence to back it up. Denying his guilt would be futile. He might as well show some dignity. There was no one so wretched, it seemed to him, as a snivelling, cowardly murderer who virtually begged to be forgiven because of the hard life he'd led or for some other daft reason. None of that for him. He'd chosen his path in life and he wasn't about to demean himself by being weak-kneed or pathetic. Why, even if the law still allowed capital punishment he would have faced the gallows with composure and some of that dry humour he was famed for. 'Just don't tie the rope as tight as I wrapped the scarf round those women,' he would tell the executioner. 'You might cause a rash.'

Not that he ever laughed at jokes made by other people about death of any description, including murder. A colleague of his at work, Mike, once took advantage of the disappearance of a child in Portugal, when her parents were briefly suspected of having murdered her, to tell the following: 'Did you hear about the woman arrested for killing her child when she was on holiday in Spain? Silly bitch should have gone to Portugal; she would have got away with it there.' Margaret, a temp, laughed loudly; others in the office smiled or sniggered. Edgar gave a shake of his head and clicked his tongue in disapproval. At times like that he came across as a bit of a wet blanket.

Curiously, that added to his popularity. He was regarded as a 'character', who, despite his apparent repugnance at the joke about the woman, never took offence at gibes aimed at himself. Indeed, he seemed to enjoy them. He could laugh at his own idiosyncrasies. Overall, it was good to have him in the office for that reason.

As for his neighbours, he cultivated a relationship with them which was distant but affable. He would exchange a few polite words on meeting any of them, but never invited any into his home. Do murderers ever do that? Do they ever invite people into their home unless they want to murder them? Edgar had no intention of killing a neighbour, so was there some psychological reason behind his reluctance – a feeling that the inside of his house was itself a murder scene already, and that he being the home owner was obviously the guilty party? The murders he'd committed must have preyed on his mind at times, and mentally must have accompanied him as he moved from room to room, doing whatever he had to do. They must have tainted the atmosphere to such an extent as he perceived it that he probably assumed that other people too would feel it and identify it as something evil. And he did have a number of books on real-life murders, such as the moors murderers and the Yorkshire Ripper; he wouldn't have wanted anyone to spot those on his bookshelf. So all in all, he preferred to keep his own company; and who could blame him, all things considered?

What anyone who visited his home wouldn't have seen was any plans for his next murder; he committed nothing to paper and stored in his head all the information he required. On the whole he followed the same routine in the way he killed his victims, so he never bothered with trying to come up with original methods; it was more a case – once his victim had been identified – of ensuring that nothing would interfere with his plan's execution. He was never nervous when carrying it out. He was confident, efficient, ruthless, and without mercy. Once he'd made up his mind to strangle whoever it was, there was no going back. Tears, terror, anguish, appeals to his humanity – they had no effect on him. Such was the case with his latest murder … of one Mabel Leach in Preston. She was eighty-four, suffering from jaundice, had yellow, wrinkled skin, was skinny with arthritic fingers, and she made funny sobbing sounds when she realised what he was about to do. But he throttled her anyway; then stealthily left the house with £465. That was all he got – apart from the thrill of doing it. For yes, he had started to enjoy the challenge more and more. It had become more important than any financial gain from it.

  Then he went home to the jigsaw. He'd left that out on the table for a couple of weeks. He still hadn't figured out what the murder was, and it bothered him. He ought to know. When he arrived home, he sat at the table, having put the murder of Mrs Leach behind him, and again tried to spot any more clues. It wouldn't have mattered if he had. A copy of *Oliver Twist* could have been lying on a chair in the picture, and he still wouldn't have guessed. He had never read the book, and all he knew about the story was Oliver's plaintive plea for more food: 'Please, sir. I'd like some more' – or whatever the line was. And such sentimentality would have been enough to put him off reading it. Now, if the jigsaw had been about a real-life murder, he was sure he would have immediately guessed which one it was.

There were no such problem this time for the staff of Fothergill Puzzles. They already knew which murder the second jigsaw depicted: Othello's of Desdemona. So as they gazed down at Gregory's painting on Mr Fothergill's table, they tended to think it was far more obvious than the first one. The handkerchief was there on the bed; the victim's face was half hidden under a pillow, suggesting she had been smothered with it; and at the edge of the picture was a hand – a black hand. Of course, for anyone unacquainted with Shakespeare it was anything but obvious, and only Chester Grounds of those present realised that that was bound to be the case. He didn't like the painting at all. His mouth was twisted in disapproval, and he now waited for the right moment to give verbal expression to his opinion.

Mr Fothergill was beaming: he liked the picture.

Melissa was wide-eyed because she thought it made her prettier than she already was. She *thought* she liked the picture.

Alysse was already weighing up how to describe the scene without giving anything away to the purchaser. It didn't matter whether she liked the picture or not: she had a job to do.

Mr Millar with an 'a' presented his usual non-committal expression to the world, so it was impossible to know whether he liked it or not.

Gregory couldn't prevent a certain pride in his work from appearing at the corners of his mouth and in the look he cast at first one person then another to gauge whether they liked it or not.

Mr Miller with an 'e' couldn't prevent a ridiculous amount of pride from appearing all over his face. He was, after all, the one who had suggested Othello's murder of Desdemona as the second jigsaw. So of course he liked the painting. He adored the painting. It seemed to him that he and Mr Dawes were partners in artistic creation. He had the idea, Mr Dawes did the painting. He turned towards Mr Fothergill, awaiting the compliment he expected. Expected and got.

'It's excellent, Mr Dawes. Don't you think it's excellent, everyone? I think we should give an especial thanks to Mr Miller for coming up with the suggestion; we might have been stuck for evermore without him.' (Expected and got in spades, so to speak.)

'Thank you, Mr Fothergill,' Mr Miller responded, 'but I think that's a bit of an exaggeration. I'm sure someone would have thought of another. Why, you yourself have suggested the murder in that Agatha Christie novel for our third jigsaw. That could have been our second one if I hadn't suggested the –'

This was too much for Chester. He interrupted his colleague.

'Do you know, Mr Fothergill? I'm not sure about that one – *The Murder of Roger Ackroyd*, isn't it?'

'Why ever not?' asked Mr Fothergill in what was almost a splutter.

'Well ...' Chester had to think quickly now. 'I think most people who are into murder stories will be expecting that one – it is one of the most famous murder mysteries.'

'Not at all. I mean, it is one of the most famous murder mysteries, yes. But there are many others just as famous. Why, Miss Christie herself has written umpteen. Don't forget *The Mousetrap* for one.'

'Why not do that?' put in Melissa, with the thrill of inspiration. 'One of the clues could be a mousetrap on the floor.'

'A bit too obvious, I think,' said Mr Fothergill. 'No, we'll stick to *The Murder of Roger Ackroyd*. I've been checking up on that and there are some really interesting clues to include. A ring with an inscription 'From R', for instance; a goose quill …'

Mention of the goose quill brought some puzzled looks from his employees.

'What's a goose quill got to with the murder?' wondered Chester out loud. 'He doesn't get killed with it, does he?' He grinned; though whether at what he thought was an amusing remark, or at the idea that anyone *could* be killed with a goose quill, was impossible to say.

Mr Fothergill raised a forefinger and gave the smile of someone who was not only a successful businessman and had married a wonderful woman with whom he was still in love, but who knew very well what part the goose quill played in the story.

'I suggest you read the novel to find out. I suggest that you all do; Miss Christie is an ingenious writer. I must confess I have thought of doing a series of jigsaws based entirely on her stories; but we've started this one and better stick to it in the manner originally conceived.'

'Or forget the *Roger Ackroyd* till we start a Christie series,' proposed Gregory, whose intervention was something of a surprise as he rarely spoke at these meetings.

'No,' insisted Mr Fothergill. 'We decided on the *Ackroyd* and that's the one we'll do. We mustn't delay in getting the puzzles into the shops, so we can't keep changing our minds.'

Chester's eyebrows shot up. *Our minds? Speak for yourself, ol' man.*

'Actually, Mr Fothergill,' broke in Mr Miller. 'I did have another idea for a murder we could use.'

'Oh?' Mr Fothergill was interested to hear what it was, but not for the third jigsaw. Only for the fourth.

'Macbeth,' said Mr Miller. 'He murdered the king of Scotland –'

'Oh, not Shakespeare again,' protested Chester. 'We might as well do a series on the murders in his plays; there are plenty of them. What about *Julius Caesar?*

Mr Miller closed his eyes in a display of superior intellect. 'Julius Caesar was murdered in real life. This is not a series of real-life murders.'

Chester glared at Mr Miller. 'I said a series on the murders in his plays; though I still don't see why we shouldn't do a series on real-life murders –'

'But we aren't doing one. If we did a jigsaw on *Macbeth*, we could use a crown as one of the clues, and a dagger … Is this a dagger I see before me, etc…'

'Actually, Mr Miller,' put in Mr Fothergill soothingly,' I think Macbeth killed the king of Scotland in real life, didn't he?'

Mr Miller's face fell, 'I thought that was a myth. I'm not sure, to be honest, now you mention it.'

Smirking, Chester put the knife in. 'Then we'd better not use it, just in case, eh, George?'

'I have to agree there,' said Mr Fothergill. 'We don't want to make fool of ourselves. So, Mr Millar … I reckon we should make this jigsaw the same size as the previous one. No reason why we shouldn't, is there?'

Chapter 6

The Second Jigsaw

There was no reason why they shouldn't, and in due course, after receiving the Mrs Fothergill seal of approval, the jigsaw was ready for delivery to any retailer ordering it. And many did. Chester found it easier than normal both over the phone and on his travels to persuade them to take double their usual order. The success of the first of the series led them to believe that the second might be as successful and even more profitable, the price having increased. They weren't wrong. The jigsaws were sold almost as soon as they were put on display. It was a phenomenon resembling the sales made by the Buzz Lightyear toy, relatively speaking. Mr Fothergill began to think of taking on more staff to cope with the extra workload.

Whenever Chester was away searching for new outlets, the phone orders had usually been taken by Alysse; but she was starting to resent having to do so much, and another sales representative seemed the right 'route to take', as Mr Fothergill expressed it when she again grumbled about it.

So another young woman, Daphne Muir, was recruited specifically to take over that role. She had short black hair and wasn't as pretty as Melissa; but she was prettier than Alysse and much prettier than Joan. She picked up the work quickly and Mr Fothergill was soon saying that he couldn't understand how they'd ever managed without her. Chester was slightly aggrieved on two accounts. First, the fact that Daphne had no car and couldn't drive anyway meant that he would spend more time travelling about than had previously been the case; and second, the fact that his advances to Daphne made no more headway than they had with Melissa, Daphne disliking toupees quite as much as the secretary did. But as Mr Fothergill told him, it would give him the chance to 'spread your wings', meaning he could visit more distant parts of the country and open new accounts there, which would be of benefit to him because of his commission and to the health of the company. Whether that in

Chester's view was preferable to bedding Daphne wasn't discussed between them.

Nevertheless, he had to admit that his commission did come rolling in. On one of his regular calls in Birmingham, a buyer assured him that *Two Puzzles and One Murder No. 1* had sold much better than Fothergill's Christmas jigsaw. Chester chuckled when he heard that. Father Christmas in that jigsaw had always seemed to him to be a little *too* merry, as if he'd opened two or three bottles of sherry which he was supposed to be delivering as presents on his sleigh. He'd said as much first to Mr Fothergill (who smiled tolerantly), then to Melissa (who giggled), then to Mr Miller (who didn't agree), then to Alysse (who cocked her eyebrow disdainfully), but realised he'd be wasting his time with Mr Millar so he'd told Joan instead, even though she hadn't seen the jigsaw (and didn't know what he was talking about).

Quite a few retailers now began to put the two *Two Puzzles and One Murder* jigsaws on display together, advertising them as a roaring success, which in truth they were. Chester played a part in that, as he'd seen the display in one shop and kept suggesting it to others, claiming that it usually led to both jigsaws being bought, if not at the same time, then within a matter of weeks. 'People who buy the first and solve the mystery can't resist buying the second to see if they can solve that one as well,' he assured them. There was some truth in that, too. It was precisely what some people had done. But there were also those who hadn't solved the mystery of the first and who still bought the second in the hope of solving that.

Edgar Rice Root, for example.

He picked it up on his travels. It must have been a case of extra-sensory perception, because he was walking along the pavement, with no intention of popping into the shop he was passing, when he suddenly felt the urge to do so. And there on display was *Two Puzzles and One Murder No. 2*. The box was similar in design to the first, though with slightly different colouring and, of course, *No. 2* instead of *No. 1* apparently increased in size by the magnifying glass. He didn't automatically take it to the cash desk and purchase it; he gave it some thought, ever careful not to betray himself for the murderer that he was. But once he'd convinced himself that the sales assistant wouldn't jump to that conclusion, he tucked it under his arm, went over to the desk and paid for it in cash, ever mindful that his credit card would leave a trail of the things he had bought.

By now he had cleared the first jigsaw from his table at home, and the first chance he got he started putting the second together. It proved more difficult than the first. There wasn't much variety in the pieces that gradually revealed the bed cover, so he had a problem finding the right fits. For most of the time, he was smoking a cigarette to aid his concentration, holding it between his thumb and forefinger when it wasn't in his mouth. He wasn't a heavy smoker. The only other times he would light up were on those occasions when he had lunch on his travels and was parked in a conveniently isolated spot, usually by a river or a canal. He often worked in such places on his murder plans. The fact that they weren't frequented by other people gave him a curious sense of exclusivity, as if that were necessary for a good plan to form in his mind. And maybe the cigarette, too, helped in that respect … even if it didn't help with the jigsaw, which it didn't seem to.

More than once – again – he felt like dumping the pieces in the bin; but with little else to do that evening he had a break for some supper and then returned to it. Even so, he didn't finish it till the next day, when the scene it revealed meant no more to him than the other had. Some woman had been suffocated with a pillow – that much was clear. But was that a handkerchief lying on the bed? Was it one of the clues? He suspected it might be, so yes, he was on the right track, and if he'd persevered along it … Well, no, he wouldn't have guessed it had anything to do with Othello and Desdemona. He had never read any Shakespeare or seen a film of *Othello*, so how could he? The murder depicted remained a mystery.

He felt frustrated and cheated. Again. And what really irked him was the realisation that some people would know which murder it was. Had he been capable of forming the words 'It isn't fair', he would have done. But that wasn't part of his mind set. In his view nothing was fair – or unfair. The world was what it was, and wasn't a game of cricket – a game that Edgar loathed. Success or failure was what mattered. One set out to do something and did it, or didn't; one succeeded or failed. One set out to murder someone, and succeeded or failed. One tried to guess which murder was being depicted in that damned jigsaw, and succeeded or failed.

He hated failing. He hated failing more than he hated the people he murdered.

He hated the people responsible for his failure. He hated *them* more than he hated the people he murdered.

And whoever had produced that damned jigsaw seemed responsible for his failure to guess which murder it depicted!

Gregory Dawes had stayed longer in the pub than he usually did. For some reason he hadn't been able to get up from his seat and leave. He felt heavy and his vision was fuzzy. If he'd been speaking to someone, he would have slurred his words. If he'd been arguing with someone he might have punched him. If he could have got his hands on that blond barmaid, he would have molested her. And there was the clue, he told himself (he tended to think in terms of clues these days): the barmaid. She was the reason he hadn't left yet. He wanted to ask her something; and when he remembered – or realised – what it was, he would. He would go over and demand an answer, and wouldn't leave until he got one. He'd fight any man in the house till he got one. He'd wreck the joint if he didn't get one. Such were the thoughts dancing drunkenly about in his brain as he again tried to focus his eyes on that rather attractive – as he perceived her from that distance – female.

In fact, she was nowhere near as pretty as Melissa, or even Daphne or Alysse, though one would have to admit she was prettier than Joan. She was overweight with bulbous cheeks, used too much make-up, and had a temper borne of having to deal too often with inebriated men … of whom Gregory was decidedly one.

Only a few other people were present, The Bay Horse being one of those gloomy public houses that had suffered a drop in clientele due to the various measures introduced by the government to curb drunken driving, measures resolutely ignored by Gregory and others of his ilk, all of whom, no doubt, would have liked to get their hands on the barmaid.

Her name was Betty, and she wouldn't have minded at all if certain of the men had succeeded in doing so. Gregory was not one of those, so when a few minutes later she saw him stumbling towards her, she picked up a clean glass and started wiping it with a dishcloth. Weirdly, doing something like that gave her a sense of security when conversing with anyone who was tipsy. Not that she expected any trouble; this particular man had visited the pub on numerous occasions without causing any bother, keeping to himself the whole time. She felt sure he was about to order another drink.

He arrived at the bar and leant on it, raised a forefinger and waggled it about.

'I want t'ask you somethin',' he slurred. 'Very important.'

'Yes, lovey – what is it?'

He waggled his forefinger again. 'Do you know … do you know … what a goose quill looks like?'

Ah! This man needed humouring.

'I can't say I do, lovey.'

Gregory raised his other forefinger and waggled that instead of the other one.

'Well, if you don't know, how can I be expected to? That's the question.'

He waited patiently for a response.

'And what's the answer, my love?'

'The answer, my dear, is that I can't. That's all there is to it. So-o-o-o … I'll have to find out. Do any of your friends know what a goose quill looks like?'

Betty was still wiping the glass.

'I could ask around,' she said. 'But I doubt it. It's not something I've previously discussed with friends.'

'Quite right, too. It's not something you should discuss with them. You might give the game away. They might guess who the murderer is.'

Murderer! Betty didn't like the sound of that. She stopped wiping the glass.

'Who is the murderer?' she managed to ask.

Gregory leered at her. 'That would be telling.' He wasn't so drunk that he didn't realise she was probably jumping to a ridiculous conclusion, so he happily proceeded with an apparent confirmation of it 'He might get caught if we mention his name. We wouldn't want that, would we?'

Betty wasn't so thick that she didn't realise now that her original conclusion *was* ridiculous.

'No, we wouldn't,' she agreed in a more relaxed tone of voice. Even so, when another man came to the bar to order a drink, she was quick to bring him into the conversation. 'You wouldn't know what a goose quill looks like, would you? Our friend here is keen to know.'

The newcomer was thirtyish, had black hair and greasy skin as if he'd just finished a hard day's work, and gave the impression that he didn't appreciate being asked difficult questions at that time of day. He shook his head.

'Can't say I do. Like a feather, isn't it?'

'Precisely,' declared Gregory. 'You've hit the nail on the head. But what kind of feather? That's the question.'

The man wasn't in the mood for a second difficult question, so he asked Betty for pint of bitter. But then some recollection stirred in his brain. 'A quill – isn't that what people used to write with?'

'Precisely,' repeated Gregory. 'You've hit the nail on the head again. But what does it look like? That's the question.'

The man shrugged. 'Like a feather. One's as good as another, isn't it?'

'Absolutely not. Can't have a feather if it looks more like a chicken's than a goose's; there has to be a difference. Where would the world be if we kept mixing things up like that?'

The man clearly didn't want to debate the issue. He picked up his drink and moved away to a table, wondering what the difference was between a prat and a pillock.

That left Betty to continue the conversation, even if she couldn't answer the question left hanging. She did the next best thing by posing a question of her own.

'So what's your interest in goose quills?'

Gregory smiled. He wasn't about to reveal any secrets.

'You heard what the man said. A quill was often used for writing. I want to practise my handwriting.' With which cryptic remark he decided to leave. Barmaids were only good for beer or bed. He'd had enough of the first and he'd lost his appetite for the second, especially after seeing her from close up (she wasn't a patch on that secretary of ol' Fothergill's).

Chapter 7

The First Letter

Joan didn't mind sitting at her desk on her own for most of the day; it gave her a sense of independence, authority and importance. The reception area was her domain and nobody else's. She was never pestered to get her work done more quickly (not that there was much to do), and no one was on hand to hear her make the numerous calls on her mobile phone – or how long they often took – when she made them from time to time. She mixed with the other employees at lunchtime in the company canteen, where she usually sat with Melissa, but never socialised with them otherwise. That would have been her choice even if it hadn't been theirs: it was one thing to have to work with people; it was quite another to want to spend one's evenings with them. One could very easily get bored of even those one liked, if one couldn't get away from them. The situation as it was suited Joan, so she had nothing to complain about. She enjoyed her job, thought her boss, Mr Fothergill, was a dear, and – unusually, according to friends who worked elsewhere – suffered no form of sexual harassment, which she felt sure would have been a bad thing.

She just wished she was prettier. She couldn't expect to be as pretty as Melissa, she realised that; but Alysse didn't always look pretty to her, and Daphne seemed rather plain – nothing remarkable anyway. Not that being pretty was so important. It was more to one's credit if one was kind and had a good personality and didn't lose one's temper the way many women did. Joan made a point of doing that: she kept her temper. Even if someone had come out and bluntly said she wasn't pretty, she wouldn't have lost it. She would have smiled and replied: 'Not to everyone, I guess.' And when someone did pass such a remark, that was what she'd say. With a smile.

Every morning, between ten and eleven o'clock, she smiled at the postman who came in to deliver the mail. She knew he didn't think her pretty, even though he hadn't said so. But he'd never ogled her and had never flirted with her, which was a dead giveaway.

'Thank you, postman,' she said with a smile on this particular day. And as usual he smiled back and went away without a word.

She didn't let that bother her. She looked through the letters and sorted them out – two for Mr Fothergill, one for Mr Miller with an 'e'. Then she rose from her chair and climbed the stairs to the offices on the second floor. Using the stairs gave her some exercise. She got precious little at any other time, and had often thought of attending keep-fit classes. It wouldn't be difficult to get fit; she was slim and healthy and never breathless. Maybe, she wondered for the umpteenth time, she should run up the stairs and see what effect that had on her. But she didn't; she never did. If Mr Millar popped out from where he worked on the first floor and saw her, he might think something was wrong and ask her what it was. He'd think her silly if she said she was just running.

Reaching the second floor, she entered Mr Fothergill's office. He was the boss, so he should have his mail first. Melissa was there. Pretty Melissa. Joan wasn't jealous (she told herself); Melissa was sweet and she genuinely liked her. Otherwise she wouldn't have sat with her every day in the canteen. It really was a case of Beauty and the Beast, she told herself. She wished she didn't, but every day without fail she did.

'Only two today,' she told Melissa, noting again how pretty she was.

'Thank you,' said Melissa, prettily. She picked up the letters, checked that they were for Mr Fothergill, then took them to him.

'Thank you, Miss Morgan,' said Mr Fothergill as she placed them in front of him.

He studied the envelopes at once. The windowed one was obviously related to business; the other ... the other filled him with excitement. It was an *ordinary* envelope! Ordinary, that is, in the sense that it was the kind that people used when sending letters to friends, letters of a more personal kind. What this one signified to Mr Fothergill was that it might be another letter from someone who had purchased one of the company's jigsaws and wanted to thank him – them – for producing something so enjoyable in the diversion it provided. He – they – had received a number of such missives congratulating him – them – on the first of *Two Puzzles and One Murder* series. Mr Fothergill hoped that this would be another, with especial reference to the second. He tore it open.

It wasn't quite what he'd expected – or at least had hoped for.

The writer did say he'd enjoyed doing the jigsaws – the *two* jigsaws – and thought the whole idea of the series was a good one; but not being a reader of fiction, he went on, he'd found it impossible to guess which murders were being 'presented for one's pleasure' (his very words). Wouldn't it be a better idea, he suggested, to produce jigsaws depicting real-life murders, which anyone who read the papers or watched the news on television would have a fair chance of identifying? 'I'm sure it would increase your sales. I'd certainly buy them.' He even mentioned a few murders that in his view would be ideal; namely, President Lincoln's assassination, Dr Crippen's murder of his wife, and the recent one of the little old lady in Preston – though he recognised that the last of these might not be as well known as the others. He signed himself Edgar Root.

Hmm, thought Mr Fothergill. Nice of him to write, of course; but he obviously didn't realise how sensitive an issue it would be to use real-life murders, even if everyone concerned was dead and buried. There were always relatives – descendants of the deceased –

to consider … which was exactly what he'd told Mr Grounds when he made the same suggestion.

Mr Fothergill always replied to his correspondents. Since they had taken the trouble to write to him in respect of the products his company sold, it was only right that he should pay them the respect of answering their concerns or showing his appreciation for their favourable comments. Either way, he was a conscientious man who took pride in good customer service. It wasn't just a matter of providing it to ensure future sales; he truly wanted his jigsaws to give his customers hours of pleasure, and if they didn't he was as disappointed as anyone.

So later that day he wrote back to Edgar Root, explaining his company's policy in respect of the *Two Puzzles and One Murder* series, and suggesting that perhaps Mr Root wasn't as sensitive as he might be to the issues regarding the use of real-life murders for the series he had proposed….

Mr Miller's letter was from the Inland Revenue, in response to one from him requesting clarification of a specific tax issue. But when Mr Miller glanced through it, his mind was elsewhere and he soon turned his attention away from it … to a séance he was due to attend that evening. He wasn't married, had never been married, and had lived most of his life with his mother, until her death three years before. Greatly – and perhaps disastrously – influenced by her in many ways, he had taken up her interest in spiritualism, and while always professing, if not convincingly, a certain scepticism, he had been a regular participant in such buffoonery for a decade. That evening, he hoped, he might receive a message from his mother from wherever she was at that particular moment. The idiot actually hoped he might.

Curiously, whereas when he had the letter from the Inland Revenue in his hand, his mind was on the séance, once he was sitting round the table with the tips of his little fingers touching the tips of two of the other idiots' fingers, his mind kept returning to the letter, wondering if the case was as clear-cut as the respondent had suggested. He was hardly aware of who was contacting whom from the realms of beyond. It wasn't *his* mother anyway. Somebody else's no doubt.

Perhaps even Dottie's. The little finger of his left hand was touching the little finger of her right hand, not for the first time during the meetings they had attended together. Was it a coincidence? Mr Miller had often wondered. Or had Dottie deliberately positioned herself in such a way that one of her little fingers would touch one of his? They were about the same age, and they had both lost their mothers in recent years. So they did have some things in common; it was only natural, he supposed, that there might be some mutual attraction, even though nothing had been said by either to the other to intimate as much. On the other hand, Mr Miller did feel more of a tingle in his little finger when it was touching Dottie's than he did when it was touching Emily's or Margaret's, say. They were both a bit older, especially Emily, who was seventy-three and looked it, with her pasty face and her frizzy grey hair hanging down past her ears without reaching her shoulders. Margaret was bonny and spoke in a confident, over-bearing voice when conversing, as if she firmly believed she was her listeners' intellectual superior. Dottie was bonny and rather shy when in company, though only for effect; she could be as bad-tempered as any of them when roused, although Mr Miller hadn't as yet perceived this trait in her personality. Had he known about it, the tingle in his little finger might have been a less pleasant experience.

He wasn't the only man sitting at the table. William Jones was the other, an amiable fool who suffered from considerable hair loss without yet being bald. He was in his sixties, complaisant in his manner, and popular with the ladies due to his interest in gardening and knowledge of flowers. But he had a comical-looking knob-like nose, which the ladies smiled at without bursting into uproarious laughter, knowing how self-conscious of it he was. His wife had died ten years before, and slowly but surely since then he had become more and more confused about life and how best to prune rose trees. Unfortunately, he made no secret of it, and insisted on asking those present for advice, a habit of his which tested the ladies' and Mr Miller's patience and always made them all the more eager for the séance to begin.

It was a ridiculous affair; yet they all went along with it. The hostess, Miriam Steele, was the medium – *professed* to be the medium. She was about forty, dark-haired, of no great physical stature, of no great mental endowments, and was a phoney through and through. Yet the idiots believed her. They *wanted* to believe her – that's the point. How could anyone believe such tosh unless they actually wanted to? So when Miriam started passing on the messages she claimed to be hearing in her head, they believed her. They all did, including Mr Miller. At times he felt ashamed for doing so. At others he would have argued angrily with anyone who expressed doubts – the doubts that he himself occasionally felt. He'd had a similar ambivalent attitude in his teens towards table tennis, which he'd played at a club for two years. His friends had often mocked him for it, so he'd never known for sure whether he actually enjoyed playing or it was just a habit he'd acquired; he didn't want to look silly in their eyes but equally didn't want to care that he did. And being overweight didn't help, since he had to wear shorts when representing his team. He had never looked good in shorts, and all that jumping about in them caused his swollen belly to wobble up and down, which badly affected his form as he thought everyone was sniggering at it; consequently he didn't win many matches. But he persevered with the game till he was studying hard for his A-levels; then he dropped it, and hadn't picked up a bat since.

Eventually Miriam appeared to collapse in a state of spiritual exhaustion, and the séance came to an end. They congratulated each other, so to speak, on achieving something, whatever they thought that was, and took their leave till the next meeting. It might have been just another day in the life of a bunch of idiots.

But it wasn't, not for Mr Millar.

For as he and the others filed out into the night through the front door, who should be passing with her new boyfriend Dave but Melissa. And she saw Mr Millar – in fact, she almost bumped into him.

It was too dark in the street for her to see how red his face turned; but his stammered greeting in response to her delighted one made it obvious to everyone in earshot how embarrassed he was.

'What brings you to this neck of the woods?' she asked – curiously, since she was more of a stranger to the neighbourhood than he was.

'An orgy, was it?' her boyfriend put in, noticing the number of females emerging from the house. He was a fit-looking man with sharply hewn features, dark-haired and wearing a black leather jacket. He'd made his remark as a joke. Whether she realised that or not, Melissa was quick to defend him.

'Oh, he doesn't do orgies, do you, George?' Every time she spoke to him and called him 'George', she always thought 'Georgie Porgie', though she'd always managed to avoid saying it.

But now Dottie intervened to answer for him.

'We've told him anytime,' she said, mischievously, as she passed them.

George Porgie gave a weak smile. No, he didn't do orgies; but he would rather have admitted to them than to séances. If he told Melissa what he'd actually been doing in the house, everyone else at Fothergill Puzzles would find out very quickly.

'Just a get-together,' he replied. 'Without the sex,' he managed to add, forcing his smile to broaden.

'That's what *he* says,' said Margaret, teasingly, as she went by, causing the smile to falter.

'So it *was* an orgy,' insisted Melissa's boyfriend.

'Hmph!' grunted George. 'I hope you're not introducing our secretary to such things.' He was fighting back, though in his eagerness to get away from Melissa he was already making to head off in the opposite direction … which was strange because his car was parked in the other one. 'I'll see you tomorrow, Melissa,' he said in farewell.

'Bye, George,' she called after him.

To his relief, she made no effort to follow him (and why should she?) but continued on her way with her boyfriend. George carried on along the pavement, feeling faintly ridiculous at moving further and further away from where he really wanted to go. He reached the corner of the street before he turned round, checked that Melissa was nowhere to be seen, and only then retraced his steps to his car. It would have been unbearable if Melissa had cadged a lift to somewhere. How could he have escaped a cross-examination then about what they'd been up to in that house? He would probably have ended up admitting everything and been a laughing stock for evermore at Fothergill's. But he seemed to have got away with it. He'd kept his cool (he told himself). How could she suspect anything like a séance? It wouldn't occur to her for a second. Orgies – that's the way her friend's mind worked, and most likely hers as well. Idiots (he told himself).

He wasn't to know that Melissa's boyfriend had brazenly asked Margaret before she got into her car. And Margaret had told him – and Melissa, because she was there listening. So Melissa had found out. She knew.

And so did everybody else at Fothergill Puzzles no later than lunchtime the following day.

Chapter 8

Secret Revealed

Fothergill's canteen was on the fourth floor, the highest in the building. The view would have been spectacular but for an equally high building opposite the windows, so it was just as well that the food provided earned the approval of virtually all the employees; otherwise many of them would have found it more agreeable to spend their lunchtimes in the nearest pub. The sandwiches on offer were varied, while the hot meals filled the largest plates and the roundest bellies. Mr Fothergill insisted on it. He refused to skimp on either the quality or the amount. Anyone who worked for his company deserved the utmost consideration, both in the workplace and during their break from it. That was his policy, and a very creditable one it was.

But he couldn't stop people gossiping while they were there, and plenty of it went on. So when Melissa settled down with Joan and a sandwich, she was soon imparting all the details of her unexpected encounter with Mr Miller in the dark street and what he and the others had apparently been 'up to' in the house. When Chester appeared, having returned to his office after finishing his travels for another week, she waved him over and, with an added air of mystery, confided in him as well.

'What do you think he was doing there?' she asked.

Chester didn't really care what George had been doing, unless it was something shocking and terrible.

'It wasn't a Shakespeare Appreciation Society, was it?'

Melissa dismissed that suggestion with a sneer and leaned closer to him, lowering her voice for no good reason, since she would happily have told everyone in the place.

'He was at a séance. Apparently he goes to them regularly. That's what one of the women said.'

Chester couldn't have been more pleased if Mr Fothergill had agreed to start a series on real-life murders. A séance! What – old George! He was conjuring up the ludicrous sight of his stuffy colleague sitting round a table with a bunch of old women (who he felt sure would be involved), when Mr Miller himself entered the canteen. He nodded to the others, went to get his food, then sat at the table next to theirs. Chester winked at Melissa. He winked at her rather than at Joan for obvious reasons. Then, after a few seconds, he turned to George and said:

'Did you say something, George?'

Mr Miller shook his head. 'No.'

Chester shook his own head, though in a more exaggerated fashion.

'I keep hearing these voices. I'm sure someone's trying to tell me something.'

Mr Miller gaped at him, scrutinising his expression. But Chester went back to his meal ... till a minute later he turned to George again.

'What was that, George? It was you, wasn't it?'

George was gaping again. 'I didn't say a thing.'

'Must be someone from the back of beyond, then … or wherever it is they float about,' said the straight-faced Chester.

Melissa and Joan, on the other hand, were trying their best not to laugh, while at the same time making it clear even to George that they were. It's having the best of both worlds, that – trying out of politeness not to laugh but showing the person who's the object of one's amusement that he is, actually, being laughed at.

George was now glaring at Chester. What he'd said had to be a reference to the séance; it had to be. And if he knew about it he could have got to know only through Melissa – though how she could have known was … no, not impossible to say. She probably knew who lived at that house; might even be personally acquainted with her, and was aware of what she did. He had been going there for years and he hadn't imagined for one second that someone he worked with might actually live in the neighbourhood, perhaps only a few doors away. If she did know Miriam, it might lead to their discussing him and –

That didn't bear thinking about. But he did think about it, and despite Mr Fothergill's policy of quality and abundance he didn't enjoy his meal at all. Chester spared him further mockery, but there'd already been enough to bother him for the rest of the day. It preyed on his mind later when he was back in his office, poring over and trying to concentrate on financial calculations. He was such a smart-aleck, that Chester. Just jealous, Mr Miller thought, because he had suggested one of the murders in the series and he, Chester Grounds esquire, hadn't. Pathetic!

He got up and went and stood by the window, gazing outside with his hands in his trouser pockets. The trouble was that Melissa might find out more from Miriam and pass all that on to Chester and everyone else. He'd be a laughing stock even if they didn't say anything to his face; though Chester probably wouldn't be able to stop himself. He'd go on making those silly comments about hearing voices. The imbecile really did think he was so funny. *I'm funnier than he is* – the thought flashed through his mind unannounced. *He's too childish to be really funny.* That did as well. *He's just a smart-arse.* That, too. He'd made sure of that one. In fact he repeated it to make doubly sure. *Just a smart-arse.*

Melissa told Mr Fothergill as well, of course. She could hardly have avoided doing so, seeing as she was in and out of his office all day.

He expressed silent surprise, but was too conscious of his employees' rights to privacy to question her. Alysse wasn't so finicky about such things, and was disappointed when Melissa couldn't provide further information. She had the utmost contempt for anyone attending séances, and felt it showed women – Melissa hadn't forgotten to tell her about them – in a bad light. As long as women believed in such stuff … well – and George! She emitted a noise that was a mixture of snort and laughter. The sad fool …

Melissa even managed to inform Mr Millar with an 'a', when meeting him on the stairs. She needn't have bothered. He nodded but gave nothing away by his expression, and didn't bother to pass it on to his assistants, who probably never did find out.

Mrs Fothergill did. It would have been surprising if Mr Fothergill had kept it from her. Why shouldn't she know? So he told her. It would have been surprising to Mr Fothergill if she'd admitted that, to be honest, she thought there might something to spiritualism. But she kept that to herself. All those years of married life, and there was still a secret between them.

*

Alysse never spread gossip at Fothergill Puzzles. She listened to it but never passed it on to anyone else who worked there. There was an element of morality in that, as if she'd learnt a worthwhile lesson from her employer. If so, it was one she forgot when in the company of friends, as was the case at a particular dinner party to which she had been invited.

'He really is the last person I would have suspected of it,' she declared to the other five people sitting round the table, none of whom suspected for a second that their doing so was what the six spiritualists had been doing at their séance, if without the tingling finger sensations. These six intellectuals, as they undoubtedly regarded themselves, were more likely to make a tingling sort of contact with each other when engaging in the cultural exchanges that were the whole point of the dinner, as Jenny, the hostess, a journalist on a women's magazine, now demonstrated.

'Have you read Norman Collins' *London Belongs to Me* yet?' She gazed round at her guests. Addressing everyone, the 'yet' suggesting that if they hadn't already read it, they were missing something of the greatest importance and should rectify the error as soon as possible. 'There's a spiritualist in that … I forget his name.

But when I was reading the passages about him I couldn't help but see Alastair Sim in the role … irrespective of how Collins described him. Just the part for him.'

Jacob Lewington was the oldest member of the group, a squat figure with wavy grey hair who liked nothing more than a night at the opera, but whose business interests revolved mainly round the art world; he was the owner of a gallery in the centre of London. He had started nodding at the mention of Collins' novel.

'I've read it – years ago. A bit pedestrian for me, as I recall, but the characterisation was well done – particularly, I agree, the spiritualist.'

'Pedestrian? Oh no, I can't agree with that,' remonstrated Jenny. She was in her element when disagreeing with remarks made at her dinner parties. It seemed to justify the invitations. What was the point of asking people to dinner if they weren't going to have discussions in which they argued from their respective positions. Agreeing with each other would have been deadly dull for all concerned and so rather demeaning. She was just about to launch into a defence of the writing, when her husband Martin interrupted.

'Wasn't a film made of it? I'm not saying Sim was in it, but I'm sure one was made.' He was tall and lean, with a bald head that he hadn't finished off in the fashion of the day by shaving off what remained of his hair above his ears. It was a statement of independence, tacitly approved of by his wife, who as a statement of her own refused to go on a diet. Not that she was grossly overweight, just a few pounds. Any more and she certainly would have gone on one, statement be damned.

'I don't know,' Jenny admitted, looking round in the hope that someone might be better informed. No one was. The other two people present were Darren, a solicitor, and Eva, a colleague of Jenny's on the magazine. She had introduced the others to Darren only recently, and it was obvious to them by now that he didn't altogether share their literary or musical interests. But he did know his Pinker and his Dennett and his Dawkins. And he went skiing, which impressed everyone. The only novels he read were those of John le Carre. Eva, on the other hand, was a writer herself, and apart from the work she did on the magazine she was building up a collection of short stories of her own for future publication. But she too hadn't read the Collins yet.

No one could confirm whether a film had been made of the novel, and Jacob soon moved the conversation on to a recent 'discovery' he had made. They were still sitting round the table, finishing their wine with the empty dishes – Jenny was an excellent cook – still cluttering it.

'Have you read *The History of a Town*?' he asked Jenny in particular.

'*The History of a Town*? I don't think I've ever heard of it.'

'By a Russian ... Blowed if I can remember his name. Shchedrin or something. Very peculiar name even by Russian standards. Contemporary of Dostoevsky.'

Jenny shook her head, mortified at not even having heard of the writer, let alone the book.

'Very original for its time. Surrealistic, some might say.'

'I have read *The Petty Demon* by Sologub.'

'And persuaded me to read it,' put in Martin. 'I hated it. She loved it.'

'It was wonderful,' cried Jenny. 'Sologub describes the people of the time so well. He –'

'He exaggerated everything. I couldn't finish it. Silly story too, if you ask me. Were we really supposed to believe that such an objectionable man would be such a capture for all those women. That's an insult to women.'

'Not at all. In those days women needed husbands far more than they do now.' This was a pointed remark, which Jenny emphasised with a curt nod in Martin's direction, which brought a smile to his face. In his view, men didn't need wives so much either.

Alysse was firmly on Jenny's side: women didn't need husbands – which wasn't quite what Jenny had said, but it was what Alysse had heard. She took comfort, too, in the fact that Jenny hadn't heard of that Russian, Shchedrin. She hadn't heard of him or Sologub. She had heard of Dostoevsky but hadn't read him. Hadn't wanted to. It was so tedious ploughing through those interminable classics from the nineteenth century. She felt the same about going to operas and the theatre; only occasionally did she feel like doing either. It was such a bore to have to go to such trouble … purchasing tickets and getting ready to go out, then sitting in a theatre listening for hours to whatever it was, music or dialogue, which more often than not wasn't worth the bother of concentrating on it.

In respect of Shchedrin and Sologub, however, she wasn't alone in her ignorance. Neither Darren nor Eva had heard of them either, so they sat back and let those who did know their work dominate the conversation, as Jenny, Martin and Jacob usually did at their gatherings.

Alysse always felt a sense of inferiority when she was with them. It was galling to her that she should be employed by a company producing jigsaws and other puzzles. It couldn't be compared – favourably – to working for a women's magazine. Jenny and Eva wrote articles for theirs on all manner of topics: she wrote promotional descriptions – blurbs (that's what they were) – for jigsaws. Jigsaws! She was ashamed of it – so ashamed that she'd never asked any of her friends whether they'd ever bought any of Fothergill's products; she would have found it humiliating to do so. Jigsaws were for children: Shchedrin, Sologub and Dostoevsky were for adults.

She lifted her glass and took a sip of her wine.

On the other hand, she mused, perhaps there was a famous murder in one of their novels which would do for the *Two Puzzles and One Murder* series. Wasn't that what *Crime and Punishment* was about? Didn't the main character murder an old woman or someone? She vaguely remembered watching a television adaptation of the novel; it would have been a simple matter to ask Jenny and the others to confirm it. Or she could go the whole hog and actually read the damned thing. Then she'd be able to tell Fothergill what clues could be used....

She drank the rest of her wine.

But was it worth it? How many people would correctly guess a murder from a Russian novel written, what, a hundred and fifty years ago? Only the likes of Jenny and Jacob, she supposed. And they didn't do jigsaws.

'Please,' she said in answer to Martin's offer of a top-up.

Chapter 9
Another Exchange of Letters

Using both hands, Edgar Rice Root cracked a walnut with his silver nut cracker. He had placed a dish underneath to catch any pieces that fell; the rest he dropped into it. Then he popped the nut into his mouth and gazed down again at the letter spread out below on the table. He wasn't happy at the reply he'd received. The respondent hadn't informed him which murders were being depicted in the jigsaws, and seemed to enjoy not doing so. It was almost as if he was poking fun at him for not knowing what they were, and at the same time accusing him of being callous – 'insensitive' – for suggesting a series on real-life murders. Edgar could see some humour in the latter, all things considered, but not in being kept in ignorance of the fictional murders.

Who was this guy? ... Andrew Fothergill – the signature was clear enough. Probably the owner, judging by his name. Someone who took pleasure in tormenting the people who bought his products. Having a laugh at their expense every day. A real sicko ...

Edgar's shoulders went up and down a few times. He was chuckling silently. *A real sicko...*

But it was annoying. If he knew in which novels the murders occurred, he could have read them and seen how well the murder scenes were represented in the jigsaws. That would have been interesting. As a professional, he liked to prepare his murders in such a way that almost nothing could go wrong – almost, because one could never guarantee it. Likewise, he expected an artist to convey a murder scene as accurately as he could, and to provide clues that were neither too simple nor too vague. An obvious clue to one of his own murders would have been a full moon shining through a window. But there would have had to be others for whoever was doing the puzzle to identify which of his murders it was ... say, a budgie in a cage so he could identify it as that of Mrs Shepherd. She was the one who'd had the budgie, wasn't she? He couldn't remember for certain. Not that the budgie had been mentioned in any of the reports he'd read. And since it hadn't, how could anyone be expected to realise it was a clue and work out from that which murder it was? ...

A clue needed to have particular relevance to the crime, in the way it was committed, or in respect of what had happened as a result of the crime, like that dog getting his legs covered in blood. That was definitely a relevant clue and so a good one. But it also had to be something that could – could – be recognised as a clue, and for that to be the case it would have to relate to a feature of the crime which was well known. The budgie wasn't. The full moon wasn't yet, since the police hadn't noticed that particular connection in the murders he'd committed.

And in the same way, if he hadn't read the particular novel in which the murder occurred, how could he be expected to know which murder it was?

It was infuriating.

Andrew Fothergill, eh ... well, Mr Fothergill, your reply wasn't acceptable. He decided he'd write again, insisting ... no, not insisting ... No, what he'd do was tell the chap that he'd been losing sleep because the mystery of the murders was preying on his mind and he needed to know so he could get some shut-eye again before he fell ill. He'd say he couldn't concentrate on his work and was in danger of losing his job if he kept making mistakes ... No, that was going too far; the chap wouldn't believe it. But losing sleep – yes, that was understandable. If the guy had any feeling for his fellow man he'd surely relent and give the information required. What could he possibly lose?

Edgar went and got his writing pad, and was soon seated at the table again, composing the letter. 'Thank you for your reply; I do appreciate it. But I do urge you to let me know ... I don't think you understand the effect that not knowing is having on me ... I'm lucky to get one night's sleep in three now ... It's silly, I know; but when something preys on one's mind as these murders are doing on mine, it just gets worse and worse ... I can assure you I won't reveal the solutions to anybody else; I wish to know only for my own peace of mind ....'

It was, he thought, a very restrained letter, very polite and, he liked to think, convincing in its description of his sleepless nights –

which was important, since that might be the deciding factor in whether the chap gave way or not.

Mr Fothergill received the letter a couple of days later. He sympathised, of course, with all that tossing and turning in bed; he'd had a few nights like that himself, when he was always frightened of waking his wife. But really … the gentleman who had written shouldn't take it so much to heart. It was only a bit of fun. Only a jigsaw. He should ask his friends if any of them knew which murders they were; that was the whole point of the series. Mr Fothergill wanted to spark people's interest in it; he was a businessman. The more people who became interested in what the jigsaws portrayed, the more people would purchase them. What Mr Fothergill couldn't do was reveal the solutions to those who wrote to him. To have done so would, he felt sure, be counter-productive. Fewer sales would result.

As he told Vera when he showed her the letter: 'People do like to make exceptions of themselves. If I told him, I'd have to do the same for anyone else who wanted to know. It wouldn't be fair to withhold from them what I've revealed to somebody else. It wouldn't be ethical. Can't sleep, he says. Huh! Not sure I believe that. He could take a sleeping pill, couldn't he? Isn't that what you've done sometimes?'

When he wrote back, he jokingly mentioned pills. 'I can assure you that if you're anything like my wife, you'll wake up as fresh as a daisy. She can't wait to get to her housework once she's had her orange juice, so maybe you'll find it easier to work out the murders once you've had yours.' A younger person might here have inserted a smiley face. Mr Fothergill didn't. But while expressing his regret at not being able to comply with his correspondent's request, he did relent a little. He provided two more clues – one for each jigsaw – to help him towards their solutions. For the first, recalling Oliver Twist's plea for more gruel, he wrote: 'You should only ask for more if you really want it'; for the second: 'If Macbeth had been found guilty of this murder, it would have been a travesty of justice'. He felt he might be giving too much away with the latter; it did seem to make it obvious that Shakespeare might be involved. Still, the poor man was obviously at a complete loss, and indeed he might be thinking in terms of a novel and have no chance of guessing which murder it was; so yes, it might be best to nudge him in the right direction.

That wasn't how Edgar saw it. When he read the letter and came to the extra clues, it became clear that previously he hadn't been, as Mr Fothergill had assumed he was, at a complete loss, because he was now. What, he wondered, was all that about asking for more? And what did Macbeth have to do with it – or *not* have to do with it, bearing mind that it would have been a 'travesty of justice' if he'd been found guilty of it. Edgar was no expert on Shakespeare; he'd never read nor watched any of his plays. All he vaguely knew about *Macbeth* was that there were witches in it. 'Hubble bubble, toil and trouble' – didn't that come from *Macbeth*? So did Macbeth murder someone … or was there a case of mistaken identity involved? Did people think he was a murderer when in fact he wasn't?

That must be it. Macbeth must have been wrongly accused but found innocent at his trial. That would tie in with what this Fothergill chap had said. There was only one way to make sure – and found out who the murderer actually was: he would have to read the play. The library was bound to have a copy; he could borrow it from there. Edgar rubbed his hands together in satisfaction. He felt he was getting somewhere. So, on his next day off from work, he went to the library and had no trouble in finding a special student edition of the play. Browsing through the pages, however, made his heart sink. He didn't look forward to wading through language like that. But what choice did he have? If he wanted to solve the puzzle of the jigsaw, he had to do it. He took the book home and spent the first part of the evening struggling to come to terms with what he was reading.

It has to be admitted he didn't digest every word; and the more pages he turned, the fewer words he even tried to understand. He wanted to get to the murder. That was his only interest. The hell with Shakespeare's poetry!

But when he reached the bloody deed Edgar was more baffled than ever (which suggests that he hadn't been at a complete loss even when he'd read the letter). Macbeth had committed the crime. Did that mean – recalling Fothergill's 'travesty of justice' – he had a good reason to murder the king and it would have been wrong to convict him? Edgar screwed his face up. Macbeth had wanted to be king – wasn't that the reason? Hardly a justifiable reason to kill the reigning monarch and be exonerated by a court of law. Even Edgar could see that while wishing to identify and sympathise with another murderer.

He closed the book with an air of dissatisfaction and sank into his armchair, pondering the plot and the outcome, and wondering what on earth any of it had to do with the second jigsaw. He'd long since put the pieces back into the box, so he'd forgotten the picture. Best, he thought, to put it together again, and see how it related to the murder in the play.

He did that straight away – or rather he started straight away. But even allowing for the greater expertise he'd acquired by having done jigsaws in the recent past, it still took him a few hours.

And, of course, the picture he looked down on once he'd finished was very hard to associate with the play he'd read.

The dead body in the picture was that of a woman.

The king in *Macbeth* wasn't a woman, for God's sake!

As for the first jigsaw and the extra clue provided by Mr Fothergill for that, Edgar was very definitely at a complete loss.

Chapter 10

Another Suggestion

Alysse too had made a visit to her local library. Curiously, considering which of the two was a murderer, she was far more furtive in her manner when doing so than Edgar. It was as though she didn't want to be recognised while she was there. More likely, she thought it demeaning that she should go to so much trouble for a jigsaw. She was looking for a copy of *Crime and Punishment*. She had decided after all to recommend the murder in it to Mr Fothergill as the next in the *Two Puzzles and One Murder* series. She wanted to see what clues she could suggest. It was almost certain that no one else where she worked had read Dostoevsky, so she had the opportunity to support her claim for a pay rise by convincing Mr

Fothergill that she deserved it. He was very appreciative of any suggestion for the products he sold, and another fictional murder for his pet series would be ideal.

She wasn't a member of the library and didn't know her way around it, so when she followed the alphabetical route along the shelves containing fiction, she was disappointed to find no copy of *Crime and Punishment*, or indeed of any Dostoevsky. All she could do, it seemed, was to ask an assistant whether one was available. She did, but reluctantly. She didn't like bringing attention to herself; it was as if letting other people know what her interests were was tantamount to revealing shameful secrets about herself. So when she asked the bespectacled, middle-aged woman behind the counter, she did so with a resentful expression on her face – a resentment which might well have increased had the woman been unable to help her. Fortunately she was able. She directed her to the shelves that contained so-called classics, and there it was in paperback.

Alysse couldn't bring herself to join the library and borrow the book, so she took it to a free seat along the rear wall and browsed through it, looking for the murder scene. When she found it, she read it almost suspiciously, as was her wont. The victim was a moneylender and a pawnbroker; the weapon used was an axe; the murderer was student; and ... he didn't kill only one person, he killed two.

The clues were obvious. One would be an axe, and a pawnbroker's sign could be shown through the window, presumably hanging above the front door; but how could one suggest that the murderer was a student? She smiled. It was the closest thing to a smile she was ever likely to give without any trace in it of cynicism: she'd imagined him with a satchel on his back. It wouldn't do, of course, but she was pleased at having thought of something so amusing.

What else? The second murder ... the head of a woman coming up the stairs could be shown through an open door. The murderer would be centre stage, the axe in his hand, so no one could doubt he was about to finish her off too.

By the time Alysse got home she had it all worked out and was ready to make her suggestion to Mr Fothergill.

She wasted no time in doing so. As absurd as it may sound, she subconsciously feared that someone else might beat her to it – might propose the very same murder. She would never have admitted that she had a self-serving desire to be the first to recommend it, but one can imagine how galling she would have found it to be the second.

She was the first – and, as a matter of fact, the only one. She responded patiently to Mr Fothergill's polite questions about her well-being, as she usually had to do when entering his office; then, in answer to his 'Now, Miss Thorson, what can I do for you?' she told him. She wasn't at her most confident in doing so, not having the greatest confidence herself in her suggestion. She got a bit flustered – uncharacteristically – when trying to remember the murderer's name (as if that mattered), but she needn't have worried.

Mr Fothergill opened his mouth wide, opened his eyes wide, both in an expression of delight.

'Why, that's a wonderful idea, Miss Thorson! *Crime and Punishment,* eh? That'll be a tricky one for them.'

'Too tricky, perhaps. That's my concern.'

Mr Fothergill snorted. 'Not at all. Dostoevsky is a very famous writer, and *Crime and Punishment* is his best known novel. There have been film and television adaptations of it; I'm sure I saw one on television once. Can't remember much of it now, but I'm certain there was. Plenty of people will know the story.'

'But are they people who do jigsaws?' Alysse wondered, seemingly determined now to dissuade Mr Fothergill from taking up her suggestion.

'Well, if they're not yet, they will be, once word gets round that our *No. 4* is Dostoevsky-related. I rather like the idea that our jigsaws are not merely amusing diversions but of cultural interest as well. It could open up a whole new market…. Ha-ha! We might start selling them in Moscow. I wonder if Mr Grounds would like a trip there. Yes, Miss Thorson, I think you've hit on a winner. I'll let everybody know about it at our next meeting. Mr Dawes is coming in with the painting for our *No. 3*. Keep it to yourself till then. I like to surprise people … when it's a pleasant surprise, that is.'

When Melissa had spread the word about George's regular attendance at séances it was Daphne's day off, so she hadn't got to hear of it for a week. For several days she was in happy ignorance of what greatly amused most of the other people at Fothergill's. When she found out, and particularly because Melissa looked astonished that she hadn't known before (as if it were her own fault that she didn't), she was deeply hurt, resentful and bitter. Being the latest recruit to Fothergill's, she felt at times she was still an outsider in the company, and something like this seemed to confirm it. As a result, she started to sulk, which did nothing for her looks. Suddenly she wasn't even as pretty as Alysse. She was still prettier than Joan, but much less prettier than Melissa than she had been before. This was unfortunate, especially as she blamed Melissa for not informing her as soon as she'd returned to work. She had even sat with her once or twice in the canteen during that week and not a word about it had crossed Melissa's lips. Hadn't she wanted her to know? Was she deliberately keeping it from her? Daphne had thought they got on well; yet Melissa seemed to have turned against her. Had she done something to cause such an attitude? She couldn't imagine what it might be. Or was Melissa jealous of her for some reason? Was it her hair style? Daphne had always been proud of her neat black hair and kept it immaculate at all times; it gave a good shape to her head. Was it her clothes? Daphne had always liked to be well dressed, and made a point of spending her money on what would generally be regarded as better quality … though Melissa was usually well dressed too, and her hair was nice as well, if she did change the colour from time to time. She couldn't work it out – and it has to be said that if she'd done the jigsaws without knowing in advance which murders were being depicted, she wouldn't have worked out any of those either.

That again wouldn't be a problem with *No. 4*, because she and the others were soon to be informed by Mr Fothergill what the murder would be.

On the day of the meeting the chosen members of staff gathered once again in Mr Fothergill's office. The first item on the agenda was Gregory's painting of No. 3, which he laid out on Mr Fothergill's table. Chester immediately wanted to know what 'that feather' was, and, when told, said it looked less like a goose quill than a feather from a chicken. Apart from that, and because no one had bothered to read *The Murder of Roger Ackroyd*, no objections were raised and everyone – apart from Chester – praised Gregory's work. The go-ahead was given and Mr Fothergill, beaming, moved on to what he assured everyone was a 'nice surprise'.

He was nothing if not conscientious in respect of the jigsaws he produced. Once Alysse had suggested *Crime and Punishment* and he had approved it, he went out and bought a copy of the novel so he could read it and know exactly what he was talking about when he presented the idea to everyone else, which he now did.

His enthusiasm came across loud and clear, but it wasn't contagious – not to judge, that is, by the facial expressions of those listening; Chester's most notably. He was the first to respond when Mr Fothergill had finished and was looking round to gauge his employees' reactions.

'Dostoevsky?' he exclaimed in exactly the same tone of voice he'd used when exclaiming 'Oh, not Shakespeare again' at a previous meeting. '*Crime and Punishment?* How many people who do jigsaws are likely to know Russian novels from the nineteenth century?'

'That's what I said,' declared Alysse, now seemingly determined to persuade everyone else that it wasn't a good idea.

'And what I said', pointed out Mr Fothergill, 'was that more people than you might assume will know them. Thanks to you, Miss Thorson, we have some good clues lined up. That axe, for instance …'

'There have been a lot of axe killers in history –' began Chester, only to be interrupted by George.

'In real life, yes. But we're not doing a series on real-life murders; you keep forgetting that, Chester.'

Chester had forgotten it and he didn't thank George for reminding him.

'I don't think many people will identify the murder on the basis of an axe,' he replied lamely.

'And the other clues,' insisted Mr Fothergill. 'The pawnbroker's sign, the woman appearing on the stairs ...'

'Hardly,' doubted Chester.

'We could' – this was Melissa – 'show a book by Dostoevsky, or whatever his name is, on a small table –'

Now it was Daphne's turn to interrupt.

'That's a bit obvious, isn't it?'

Melissa was taken aback by the spite in Daphne's dismissal of her suggestion. But she didn't have time to dwell on it. Mr Fothergill's face had lit up; he raised a hand to silence everyone.

'Indeed, it is,' he agreed. 'But you know, it's given me an idea – a rather cunning one. We could show a book by Tolstoy on a table. It would be a red herring. Imagine what will happen. People will assume that the murder happened in one of *his* novels. The clue will be there, but only in the sense that it points to the murder taking place in a novel by a Russian writer – not necessarily Tolstoy.' He looked around again at his employees.

There wasn't much difference in their expressions. Virtually everyone had a furrowed brow and puckered lips indicative of doubt. Mr Millar with an 'a' was one exception, as might be expected, his brow unfurrowed, his lips unpuckered, his visage a blank. Melissa had lowered eyebrows instead of a furrowed brow which might have been her own sceptical response to Mr Fothergill's suggestion, or her puzzled reaction to Daphne's attack, which she had perceived as such.

'Won't that make the murder even more difficult to work out?' queried Chester.

'What's wrong with that?' Mr Fothergill demanded. 'Let's put our customers to the test. Why, it might be even better to make our jigsaws harder. Imagine how our sales might be boosted if intellectuals start taking an interest.'

At the mention of intellectuals, Alysse couldn't help thinking of Jenny and the others. Jigsaws … Jenny? … Jacob? … Unlikely.

Chester was of a similar mind, but he felt he'd objected enough for one meeting, so he fell silent. And since no one else had anything to say in opposition to Mr Fothergill's latest brainwave, the meeting came to an end shortly afterwards; though not before Mr Fothergill insisted they all give thanks to Miss Thorson for coming up with such a marvellous idea. Most of them nodded in dutiful appreciation, but only Melissa actually spoke.

'Thank you,' she said.

As they filed from the office, led by George, Chester called out to him.

'Did you say something, George? I thought I heard you muttering.'

George's head swung round; he was fully aware that this was another of Chester's gibes. Then inspiration seized him.

'Really, Chester – that wig of yours is full of dandruff. Don't you ever wash it?'

A nice riposte, if one not appreciated by the wearer of that particular hairpiece.

Chapter 11

Enmity Achieved

A nice riposte indeed. George regarded it as such, and kept repeating it to himself for the rest of the day. To see the look on Chester's face when he'd said it was worth all the mockery he'd had to endure. And if Chester persisted with his silly jokes about hearing voices, he knew one or two other things he could say in retaliation. 'What's that beaver doing on your head, Chester – building a dam?' … 'Is that rat laying eggs on your head, Chester?' … Yes, he was fully armed now for their next confrontation.

Chester was equally determined to be ready. George's words kept repeating themselves in his head too, and he didn't like to be bested in witty repartee. Actually he didn't think George's remark was particularly witty, but he'd sensed that those around him who heard it did; he didn't see anyone smirking but he'd sensed that some of them were. He didn't like it and he wasn't one to take it lying down. He had always been prepared to go to extraordinary lengths to get the better of another person, either in fun or in bitter revenge. It wasn't entirely clear even to him which it would be in this case, but he soon had an idea how to have his fun or to exact revenge, whichever it was.

The relationship between Melissa and Daphne likewise continued to deteriorate, in their case into a kind of simmering suspicion of each other. Melissa was still mystified by Daphne's attitude, which now declared itself in her refusal to catch the other's eye at every opportunity, even when surface-polite words were exchanged between them. Melissa reciprocated by turning away from Daphne as soon as she realised that Daphne had not even started looking at her. They avoided each other whenever they could. That was easy most of the time, working as they did in different offices; but in the canteen they now made a point of choosing to sit at different tables.

It wasn't long before the other members of staff became aware of what was going on. Naturally, Chester made some sport of it. Whenever he was sitting at a table with Melissa, he would suddenly look over to Daphne and say to Melissa: 'I think Daphne wants you', and when Melissa turned towards her: 'Oh, no. My mistake.' And whenever he was sitting with Daphne, he would suddenly look towards Melissa and say to Daphne: 'I think Melissa wants you', and when Melissa turned towards her: 'Oh, no. My mistake.' That sort of thing kept him amused for a week or two, and did nothing to reconcile the two women. As their irritation with his facetiousness grew, so too did their resentment of each other, as if the very presence of the other was the cause of Chester's silliness.

Melissa told her mother about the tension between her and Daphne. She lived at home, despite having planned for a year or two to move out, since the tension between her and her mother was even worse than it was between her and Daphne; only the high rents for flats in London had prevented her from leaving before now. Her mother, still an attractive woman at fifty years of age, though never as pretty as her daughter, was appropriately sympathetic. Melissa was her daughter and if she couldn't side with her against a young woman she'd never met, she firmly believed she didn't deserve to be called a mother. Whoever was in the right didn't matter; she would have supported her daughter even if she was in the wrong. As it happened, once she heard how Daphne had suddenly turned against Melissa for no apparent reason, she was adamant that she, Daphne, was jealous. 'Just jealous,' she repeated, with a sneering expression that appeared on her face whenever she used the word. 'Probably because of your looks. Is she pretty?' – 'She's quite pretty, yes,' replied Melissa. – 'But not as pretty as you,' insisted her mother. 'That's what it is. Some young women are like that. They can't stand it when other women are prettier than they are. It's jealousy; that's all it is.' All of which mollified Melissa and made her feel even prettier, even though she didn't altogether accept what her mother had said.

Daphne told *her* mother, who wasn't as attractive as Melissa's mother. She was still living at home, though she had no plans to move out as she and her mother got on very well and confided in each other all the time. When her mother heard the type of person that, according to Daphne, Melissa was, she immediately insisted that she, Melissa, obviously thought a lot of herself. 'Is she pretty?' she asked. – 'She's very pretty,' admitted Daphne. – 'That's what it is. Young women who are very pretty think they can laud it over everyone. It's because all the men drool over them. Is that what the men do at Fothergill's?' – 'Some of them do, yes.' – 'There you are. That's what it is. You've done nothing wrong, Daphne. Pay no attention to her. She'll soon stop paying no attention to you.'

Had Mr Fothergill been aware of the ill will building up between Melissa and Daphne, he would have brought them together and had a heart-to-heart talk with them. He hated disharmony in his company. To have two or more of his employees at loggerheads could affect their efficiency and the smooth running of the business. It was always best, he believed, to nip such things in the bud. At the moment, however, his mind was taken up by *Two Puzzles and One Murder No. 3* and *Two Puzzles and One Murder No. 4*. He was constantly in touch with Mr Millar with an 'a' to see how production of *No. 3* was progressing, and, unusually, he had phoned Gregory more than once to urge him to complete his painting for *No. 4* as soon as he could. He wanted to maintain consumer interest in the series by getting both jigsaws in the shops within weeks rather than months. Christmas was approaching, and two new jigsaws on sale would be better than one, especially as many people had shown such a liking for the series that they were bound to buy both.

There were no hitches in respect of *No. 3*. That was in the shops by late October, by which time Melissa and Daphne had achieved a true enmity by not talking with each other, thinking the worst of each other, and making unkind remarks about each other to various colleagues, if in a way that didn't reveal that they themselves were being nasty. Daphne was good at that, Melissa not so good.

The most awkward moments for the pair were whenever Daphne called in to see Mr Fothergill. The conversation followed similar lines, depending on whether Mr Fothergill had asked her to come or she had a reason of her own to come. For instance, on one occasion:

'I'd like to see Mr Fothergill.' Daphne wasn't looking at Melissa when she said this.

'Have you an appointment?' Melissa, having seen who had entered her office, looked down at her desk and moved some papers about as if she was sorting them out because they were important.

'No, but –'

'I'm sorry. He's very busy at the moment. Can you come back later?'

'I need to speak to him now.'

'About what?'

They still weren't looking at each other.

'Matters he'll be interested to hear about. They are important.' Knowing all about pretending that something was important when it wasn't, Melissa pulled a face. Nevertheless she had a good line here and she wanted to use it.

'I'll go and see if he has any time for you.' It was one of her better attempts at being snide.

With a great show of reluctance, she got up and went in Mr Fothergill's office, returning almost immediately, with another show of reluctance.

'You can go in. But don't keep him long. He has a lot of business to attend to.'

And so with a bit of a smirk on her face Daphne gained access to her employer, feeling that she had got the upper hand over her enemy.

Melissa smirked to herself, pleased to have given Daphne so much trouble before allowing her to go through.

Mr Fothergill could have been forgiven a smirk or two once *Two Puzzles and One Murder No. 3* was in the shops. Sales in the first week massively exceeded expectations, and were three times those of *No. 2*. The jigsawing fraternity had taken to the series in a big way. It was very gratifying.

But no, not a smirk crossed his features. He wasn't a man to smirk. Just a gentle smile of satisfaction which encompassed his praise of those members of staff who had helped to make the series such a success – that was all he allowed himself … until, that is, a few days later, when he received another letter from Mr Root of Blackpool.

Then his smile became one of rueful sympathy. Mr Root seemed to have so much trouble working out which murders were being depicted; and here he was again, having just as much difficulty with *No. 3*. It was sad really. Getting less sleep than ever, he claimed. Mr Fothergill still found it hard to believe he was actually being kept awake. But how marvellous that the gentleman should think so highly of the jigsaws that he was desperate to solve them! Mr Fothergill shook his head – he actually shook his head. As sympathetic as he was to Mr Root's frustration, he wasn't about to relent and give him the answer he desired. On the other hand, he couldn't ignore him. He would have to send him another additional clue – even though his others hadn't seemed to help him much, since he still hadn't worked out the murders shown in the first two jigsaws. Better make the next additional clue an easier one. Mr Fothergill started racking his brains. But it was only when he discussed it with his wife later that he – or, rather, she – came up with a good idea that was also quite simple: an anagram – of 'Agatha Christie'. Once Mr Root worked it out, he would know who the author of the novel was. Then he'd find the murder much simpler to identify.

At first Mr and Mrs Fothergill found it far from simple to use all the letters in Ms Christie's name when trying to string words together sensibly. They would start from a word like 'great' and search for others in the remaining letters to go with it, like 'his great cat'; but that still left 'h', 'a' and 'i', and no amount of manipulation could make sense of those three letters. They tried 'hairs' and 'tears' and 'star' with a similar lack of success. Eventually they arrived at 'Agh I hate this car', and for a few minutes they thought they'd got what they wanted … till Mrs Fothergill pointed out that there were three 'h's in it – one too many. But a quick erasure of one of the 'h's and a removal of the 't' from 'this' to the end of 'car' resulted in 'Agh I ate his cart'.

It wasn't ideal, but it was an anagram, and anagrams didn't have to make too much sense. So that was the one they settled on, and that was the one Mr Fothergill sent off the following day with a letter thanking Mr Root for his continued interest in Fothergill's jigsaws and advising him that *Two Puzzles and One Murder No. 4*, would be in the shops within a couple of weeks.

To say that *No. 4* would be available then was optimistic, but Mr Fothergill had faith in Gregory to finish his painting, in Mr Millar's production team to get the jigsaw cut, and in the company's distribution team to deliver within days to retailers around the country the boxes containing them. He wasn't disappointed. Gregory brought his painting in that very week.

The first thing that Mr Fothergill looked for as he gazed down at it was the red herring – the book by Tolstoy. It was there, with the name 'Tolstoy' writ large on the spine. The pawnbroker's sign could be seen through the window, and the head of a woman coming up the stairs could be seen through the open door.

'An excellent piece of work, Mr Dawes,' said Mr Fothergill, who immediately asked Melissa to round up the usual members of staff for them to inspect 'our latest masterpiece'.

Melissa did so, making a point of telling only Chester when she called on him, perhaps in the hope that Daphne, who shared his office, wouldn't know that she was expected as well. A vain hope, for Daphne did come, if only to foil Melissa in her underhand tricks.

Truth to tell, the painting wasn't one of Gregory's best. That was plain to see for most of those who now, having arrived, peered down at it. There was little point in criticising it; Mr Fothergill wanted it in the shops before Christmas, and to have asked Gregory to make improvements would have made that unlikely, if not impossible. So they dutifully nodded their heads in mute approval, and Mr Fothergill, rubbing his hands together as he usually did at such moments, gave the go-ahead.

At which moment Chester spoke up.

'Oh, Mr Fothergill; I've had an idea.'

Mr Fothergill was all for new ideas, so Chester went on.

'I think we've been neglecting board games of late. We've been doing so well with our jigsaws that we've overlooked the potential sales from new board games.'

Mr Fothergill pulled a face. 'Well, yes, but computer games have taken over the market for games.'

'To an extent, yes; but I'm thinking of a game for very young children who haven't grown up enough yet to be able to use computers. I can imagine four or five of them sitting round the board, having a wonderful time. Do you remember those 'Magic Robot' games, when a robot would answer questions you asked it. I imagine it as something similar to that. We could call it 'Séance', because that's what it would be – a game for kiddies who play at holding a séance, asking questions of the dead. It'd be great fun.'

Mr Fothergill didn't immediately grasp what everyone else had grasped: that Chester was poking fun again at George, who, scowling, had certainly grasped it and would have liked to do his colleague serious physical injury, had he been holding the axe in the painting.

Grins and sniggers from some of those around him made Mr Fothergill aware that there might be more to Chester's suggestion than he had initially thought.

Oh, yes … séances … Mr Miller with an 'e' attended séances … Mr Grounds was having a bit of fun at Mr Miller's expense….

It was not the sort of thing he approved of. Best to pretend he still hadn't got the joke.

'I'll think about it, Mr Grounds. Thank you very much for the suggestion; I'm always happy to consider new ideas.'

All of which brought a few grins and sniggers at his expense as well.

Chapter 12

Getting Somewhere

Edgar Rice Root, his head bowed over the table, gazed down at the latest letter from Mr Fothergill. Actually, it was more of a gape than a gaze. He couldn't make head or tail of the additional clue that the chap had provided. 'Agh I ate his cart' – what in God's name was that all about? 'If you sort it out, you'll be some way to solving the murder' – that was what he'd written. What cart? There was no cart in the jigsaw. Edgar growled in frustration. It didn't make sense. Why would anyone eat a cart? Was it a chocolate cart? 'Agh I ate his cart.' How could a sentence like that relate to the jigsaw?

Edgar didn't do crosswords. If he did, he would have realised at once that all he had to do was to rearrange the letters to find the clue. It would have spared him more suffering. For that's what it now was – suffering. He suffered from not knowing any of the murders depicted; suffered the difficulty of not getting to sleep too easily (he hadn't been exaggerating too much in his letters to Mr Fothergill); suffered the humiliation of knowing that other people around the country – perhaps in their thousands – had guessed which murders they were. It didn't matter that he never read fiction: he wanted to know what the damned murders were. The jigsaws should have been about *real-life* murders!

'Agh I ate his cart' – ridiculous …

And yet … within twenty-four hours he was on the right track. Almost as a last resort, he decided to ask Mike in his office if he could make any sense of it. He wrote out the words, and challenged him. Mike accepted the challenge and, ten minutes later provided the answer.

'Agatha Christie.' He'd thought it so easy that he couldn't be bothered sounding triumphant.

Edgar merely said: 'Well done', as if he had known the answer and was only putting Mike to the test. He didn't explain why.

Mike thought it odd but, finding Edgar odd as well, couldn't be bothered enquiring.

Edgar called in at the library before going home. Even he had heard of Agatha Christie, and knew she wrote murder mysteries. He was getting somewhere. She was obviously the author of the novel in which the murder occurred. If the library had a copy of the book, he could borrow it and make sure that everything tallied with the jigsaw. If it didn't, he would write a different kind of letter to that Fothergill chap, criticising his company for issuing a very inferior product.

He soon located the shelves containing fiction, only to be disappointed at not finding anything by Agatha Christie under 'C'. Very quickly, however, he realised there was a special section for crime novels, and there under 'C' was *Death on the Nile*. He browsed through it. Somehow he didn't think this was the novel he needed. It was set in Egypt – and that was not the impression he got from the jigsaw. At first he couldn't even find where or when the murder was committed; but when he finally did, after about fifteen minutes, he knew it wasn't the right book: the murder was committed on a boat going down the Nile, not in an English country house, where he'd always assumed the murder in the jigsaw was.

He slipped the book back in its place, deciding to ask an assistant whether the library held any other books by Agatha Christie. He went to the counter. A young woman was there, with long wavy red hair, a floral-patterned skirt down to her ankles, and a ring in her nose. How he would have like to throttle her there and then! He hated young women who wore rings in silly places like that. But this wasn't the time …

He made his enquiry. 'You do have that one about the Nile, but I think I've read that.'

'Yes, I've read it too. It's good, isn't it?'

'Oh, you read Agatha Christie, do you? Have read any others?'

'Only a few. One of the Miss Marples and *The Murder on the Orient Express.*'

'Do you have those in the library?'

'We do, yes. We have six or seven altogether.'

'Tell me – does any of them contain the feather of a chicken as a clue?'

'The feather of a chicken?'

'A chicken feather, yes.'

The assistant went through the motions of puzzled thinking.

'I don't think so. No – definitely not in the ones I've read.'

'Are the others available?'

'I'll check.'

She did so, using her computer and keeping him informed of her findings the whole time. After a few minutes:

'The only two we have in the library at present are *The Mysterious Affair at Styles* and *And Then There Were None*.'

Edgar nodded. 'They'll do.'

She went and got them, while Edgar waited by the desk, wondering if *The Mysterious Affair at Styles* was the more likely to be set in a country house. It would seem so, judging by the title. 'Styles' sounded like the name of a country house. Nevertheless he borrowed both books – and looked forward to reading them.

And read them he did. He devoured both over the weekend. But not a single chicken feather did he find in either. He quite enjoyed them, but still felt frustrated at being no nearer to the solution of the murder in the jigsaw than he had been when he started them. How many more Agatha Christie novels would he have to read before he found the right one?

He decided to wait till the following weekend before returning the books; by then there might be another one available. But by then too, still none the wiser, he'd worked himself up into quite a state. The jigsaws should be depicting REAL-LIFE murders! Why should he have to read lots of novels just to find out what a stupid jigsaw was a picture of? And one fine dark evening, as he took a stroll along the front towards the cliffs where'd committed his first murder, he had a rather amusing idea. At least, *he* thought it amusing. He gazed out over the sea as he pondered it. The water was black, apart from where white breakers ran gently and almost silently onto the sand. But he was hardly aware of those. The jigsaws should be about real-life murders. They *would* be about real-life murders! That was his amusing idea. All he needed to make them about real-life murders was to repeat the clues in the jigsaws – to leave clues on a murder scene which matched the clues in one of the jigsaws. A dog with bloody feet, a handkerchief … a chicken feather. There was a little old lady in Leyland … he'd been planning to murder her. And he would – as soon as he'd bought the necessary items to replicate the clues in the first jigsaw.

Of course, he wasn't about to lumber himself with a real-life dog. He bought a fluffy doll dog, with the intention of painting the feet red. He wasn't sure what he'd use as a club to batter the woman, but anything heavy would do. He'd leave that in the fireplace once the deed was done. What else was there? Well, what he intended to do was to leave the clue of a full moon. That would be a clue to the murders he had already committed. He wasn't sure when the next full moon was due, and he didn't want to wait till then, so rather than do so he might just as well leave something to indicate it. But what? … A calendar … with the date ringed of the next full moon … without explanation. That would puzzle the police. Edgar chuckled. They'd be as puzzled as he had been when trying to work out the murders from the completed jigsaws. It was as good a way as any. So he bought a calendar as well – one that mentioned the dates of the full moons. For the murder corresponding to the second jigsaw – he was already planning a series – he would use a calendar that *didn't* mention the dates of the full moon. He would still ring the date on which the next one was due, to see how clever the police were. They wouldn't know that the murderer had done it; they might think the victim had, for whatever reason she had.

Edgar was becoming extremely enthusiastic about the whole project. Curiously, once he'd definitely made up his mind to go ahead with it, he rubbed his hands together, exactly as Mr Fothergill had done on more than one occasion. If one had looked at only their hands when they did, it would have been hard to tell the murderer from the manufacturer.

After what happened at Fothergill Puzzles that week, it would have been hard to tell the murderer from the sales representative.

A parcel arrived for Chester Grounds. It was tied up in Christmas wrapping paper, with a card on which was written: 'For everyone at Fothergill's – for the hours of pleasure you have given me.' There was no signature, and how curious, thought Joan, who accepted the parcel, that it should be addressed to Chester. Did he have a secret admirer? But the card stressed that it was for everyone at Fothergill's, so she thought it only right that everyone should know and that everyone should be present when Chester unwrapped it. She took it to Chester, but told Daphne not to let him open it till everyone was there. Chester was only too happy to comply. He couldn't imagine who had sent him a gift, and he passed the time waiting for the others in trying to guess who it might be.

Before long, Mr Fothergill turned up, with Alysse, Melissa, Mr Miller and Mr Millar close behind. Mr Fothergill actually rubbed his hands together again in anticipation of what the parcel contained.

'Come along, Mr Grounds, don't keep us waiting.'

Chester cut the string with a pair of scissors and started tearing off the wrapping. At this point, it should be mentioned that George's expression was as sober as Mr Millar's. Not a flicker of amusement could distinguish his from the production manager's. Nor did it change by as much as a flicker when the 'gift' was revealed.

A box of thirty Velcro hair curlers.

Daphne and Melissa sniggered. Mr Fothergill tried not to grin but failed. Alysse tried to chuckle but couldn't quite manage it. Mr Millar came as close to a smile as he ever had since starting with the company. Chester seethed. Chester grew red in the face. Chester sought out George with venom in his eyes. George's expression still hadn't changed, but sensing that Chester was glaring at him he raised his eyebrows in a show of surprise – which fooled no one, least of all Chester. He knew who had sent the curlers – curlers addressed to him, but 'for everyone' so that everyone else would be there when he opened the parcel.

He did his best. He strove manfully to overcome his mortification and take it in his stride.

'Not very funny,' he declared – which brought more sniggers from Daphne and Melissa. 'Still, they are for everyone, so I'd better share them out. Here you are, Daphne, five for you –'

'I don't use them.'

'Well, five for you, Melissa. Or do you want more? You can have Daphne's share if –'

'I don't use them either.'

Alysse was already shaking her head.

George was already leaving the room.

'Just make sure you keep some for your own hair, Chester,' he called out as he opened the door. 'It'll look a lot better with a few waves in it.' Then he stepped outside and shut the door behind him.

Much better, he thought, than that beaver joke.

*

As Melissa left the office, she glanced at Daphne and shook her head with a smile. It was an acknowledgement that she and Daphne had shared a snigger at Chester's silly toupee. Daphne responded with a shake of her head and a smile. They were suddenly friends again at Chester's expense. By the end of the week they were even talking about sharing a flat together. When Daphne told her mother, she had to weather a storm of abuse.

'You've always been selfish,' her mother berated her. 'No matter how hard I've tried to bring you up, you've never appreciated it. When you have children of your own, you'll realise what it's like, being at a child's beck and call the whole time and being taken for granted. Then you'll be sorry. I always knew you'd move out eventually; I've had to live with it for years. But have I ever tried to make you feel guilty? No – never. And do you thank me for it? No – you don't. You suddenly turn round and tell me you're moving out. Well, go. See if I care….'

And so on.

*

Edgar Rice Root might have been doing Daphne a favour if, instead of murdering the little old lady in Leyland, he had finished off her mother. But no, it was the little old lady in Leyland who fell foul to his ambitious project.

Chapter 13

Two Police Investigations

It was a messy murder scene. Edgar had used a home-made club to put an end to the woman's lonely life. There was plenty of blood lying about, and how ironical that Inspector Fullerton, who was in charge of the investigation, should have got some on his shoes, bearing in mind the fluffy doll dog sitting on the armchair as though in witness to what had occurred. The inspector saw it but thought nothing of the red feet, assuming that since it was a doll it could have had feet of any colour. And why should he have paid any attention to it when the murder weapon was there, propped up against the gas fire? There was no doubt but that it was the weapon; the blood and some strands of the victim's hair sticking to it made it easy to identify. He missed the significance of the calendar pinned to the wall. For all he knew, that could have been there all year, so he could hardly be blamed for not noticing that the date of the next full moon was ringed.

Frederick Fullerton's nickname in the service was 'Ted', which was used affectionately, sarcastically, or contemptuously, depending on the user's attitude towards him. He was diligent or careless, perceptive or blind to the obvious, genial or bad-tempered, depending on which side of the bed he'd climbed out of. He was a large man, with broad shoulders, a thug-like face, and strong meaty hands. He wasn't one to get physical with. But he had a brain, when he had a mind to use it, even if he didn't always use it as well he might have done when he did.

He spent two hours looking for clues. The forensics team had found no fingerprints, and it wasn't immediately apparent that anything had been taken from the house. Fullerton assumed that money had been stolen, but even that was by no means certain.

'Why would anyone batter an old woman like her unless he wanted something very badly?' he asked Detective Sergeant Carter, not expecting an answer – not expecting a *sensible* answer, at any rate; he didn't think much of Carter's abilities in that respect. 'But what? He hasn't touched the purse in her handbag. Not that there was much in that. Did he find a wad of notes somewhere else? You know what some of these old ladies are like … frightened of trusting banks. It's a puzzle, Carter – a real puzzle.'

'Perhaps he's just a sicko who likes beating up on old women,' suggested Carter.

'Please don't use Americanisms to me, Carter. "Beating up on" is an Americanism. You don't need the "on". "Beating up" will do perfectly well.'

Carter gulped with embarrassment. He was a youngish man for the position he held, and liked to think he'd been promoted on merit; yet Fullerton was always correcting him for one thing or another, pointing out clues he'd missed and criticising his research methods. So he made another suggestion.

'You don't think he's the same man who murdered that woman in Poulton-le-Fylde, do you? He –'

'Why should you think that? That woman was strangled. This one has been battered with a club. Hardly the same method of killing her, is it? Come on, Carter, tell me what similarity is there between the two?' He was goading him now.

Carter's face turned red. He hadn't really thought it out, and no, he couldn't immediately see any connection between the two – except that the victims were elderly women. So … stupidly:

'The victims were both elderly women.'

Fullerton's scorn was so great that he didn't even reply. He resumed his search round the house for clues – and again ignored the fluffy doll dog with red feet and the calendar pinned to the wall. It would have been a feather in Carter's cap if he had drawn attention to either of them. But he didn't. They meant no more to him than they did to his superior.

Edgar Rice Root would have been amused, if not a little disappointed, had he known how the police had overlooked the clues he had planted. Amused, because he realised how baffled they must have been (exactly as he had been by the jigsaws), but disappointed because they would, he felt sure, have been even more baffled if they'd spotted them and been at a loss to explain them.

What's more, when he purchased and then put together *Two Puzzles and One Murder No. 4*, he felt he was getting better himself at spotting clues in the jigsaws. There was one in *No. 4* that, in his view, could not be missed: the book by Tolstoy on the table. Clearly, he reasoned, the murder occurred in a novel by Tolstoy. And he had a good idea which one it might be: *War and Peace*. Even he knew Tolstoy had written that. It was one of the most famous books in the world. And that pawnbroker's sign – there must be a scene in *War and Peace* involving such a sign. Maybe the murder – with that axe, presumably – took place at a pawnbroker's. It must have done. Edgar might well have rubbed his hands together at this point. But he didn't. He clasped them instead and held them under his chin as he leaned forward on the table, gazing down at the jigsaw. *War and Peace* – the library was bound to hold a copy of that....

As indeed it did; though Edgar's heart sank when he saw the size of it. There was enough novel there, he thought, for five or six murders. Over a thousand pages! Hard to see how a writer *couldn't* put five or six murders in a novel that long. He didn't exactly look forward to ploughing through it, but he borrowed it and started reading it as soon as he got home.

Two days later he'd reached page 15.

He picked up speed over the next week, but only because he was missing out whole sentences and even paragraphs. He took the book with him on his travels and parked now and then simply to read another chapter. And slowly but ever so slowly he did make progress, even if he did have hundreds of pages to go.

At some point during the first half of the novel, he started growling to himself. There were so many characters in it he kept losing track of which was which. And all that stuff about that silly young woman being in love ... it wasn't to his taste at all and wasn't what he was looking for.

But he kept looking ... kept reading for another week; he spent every evening reading it. There was a duel ... but not a murder; and the duel resulted in only a wounding, not a killing. His growling increased. Whenever he needed to rest his eyes, he slammed the book shut in irritation; he hadn't come across a pawnbroker yet, let alone a murder. But before long it was back to the book and more reading for another week. What was this – Pierre, one of the leading characters, wants to assassinate Napoleon? Was that going to be the murder? Was that how Napoleon died in real life

– in a pawnbroker's? Edgar frowned. Somehow he doubted it. But now he read avidly, another hundred pages. No, God damn it, suddenly the French were sacking Moscow and killing hundreds – and none of them in a pawnbroker's!

Then he reached the last part of the novel. Four weeks it had taken him to get there. His eyes were unblinking as he stared down at the page. They were red and bleary with the effort he'd put in. And he still had that last part to get through. He flicked through the pages, looking for any mention of the word 'pawnbroker' or for any suggestion that a murder was taking place. There was none. None of either. He closed the book as gently as only a man feeling vicious could do. He had wasted his time. There was no murder in this damned book corresponding to the murder scene in the jigsaw. None.

Edgar felt positively murderous. There was nothing unusual in that, but there was a nastiness in it which he seldom felt even while carrying out his executions. There was also a nagging fear that he might have missed the scene describing the murder. He hadn't read every single word or every page. The horrible idea that he ought to glance through the novel again was hard to stomach. He wouldn't do that. He'd murder someone else instead. The murder in the second jigsaw. It was time to replicate that. So he did. He'd already selected the 'lucky lady', as he amusedly liked to refer to her. She lived in Chorley; so one wintry evening, a few days before Christmas, off to Chorley he went with his Christmas presents – as he amusedly liked to refer to them – of a calendar and a white handkerchief.

He used her own pillow – though truth to tell he used his hands to strangle her, before carrying the body up to her bedroom, where he dumped it on the bed. Then he placed the pillow on top of her face, put the handkerchief in her hand, and pinned the calendar to the wall above the bed, with, as usual, the date of the next full moon ringed in red ink.

The following day, he returned *War and Peace* to the library. Despite his murder of the woman in Chorley, he was still vexed that he hadn't solved the mystery of *Two Puzzles and One Murder No. 4*. What possessed him as he handed the book to the assistant, heaven knows, but he found himself asking whether the library carried any other novel by Tolstoy.

'Oh, yes,' replied the same young woman who had helped him before. '*Anna Karenina*. I've just put that back on the shelves. With the classics. Over there,' she pointed out with a forefinger.

Edgar could have done without the finger. Something about it annoyed him. He couldn't have said what it was, but he could have throttled her on the spot for using it like that. But he crossed the room to the indicated shelf and, sure enough, there was a copy of *Anna Karenina*. His face fell. His heart plummeted. It was almost as long as the other one. Tentatively he drew the book out and flicked through the pages, hoping to see the word 'pawnbroker' flashing like a neon. To no avail. Of course, to no avail. But he wouldn't be denied. There had to be a murder in it. And he'd find it. He would. So he borrowed the book and started reading it as soon as he got home.

By Christmas Day he'd reached page 15.

By Christmas Eve, the body of the woman in Chorley had been found by her daughter. Inspector Fullerton was called in to investigate. He was accompanied by Detective Sergeant Carter. The forensics team had found no fingerprints.

'A nasty business,' Fullerton muttered to his colleague.

Carter nodded. 'Not a nice Christmas present for the daughter.'

Fullerton glared at him. 'I can do without stupid attempts at being witty, Carter. We're investigating a murder, not the theft of marzipan from a sweet shop. There are two things I can't stand: Americanisms and stupid attempts at being witty. Spare me both, will you – or resign from the force. Make up your mind before we leave this house.'

Carter's face went pale. Fortunately he resisted saying something else that he found funny: that because the woman was holding a handkerchief in her hand, she was probably blowing her nose when the murderer struck. If he'd said that, Fullerton would probably have *thrown* him out of the house.

Fullerton was peering at everything very closely, trying to recognise any clue that was lying about. But he didn't see that the handkerchief was a man's large one, not a small one of the type used by old ladies. Nor did he spot the significance of the pillow on the woman's face. And he hardly glanced at the calendar, though it did catch his eye on the wall at the head of the bed. An unusual place, that, for a calendar. Still, old ladies could be eccentric.

On the other hand, he did have a weird feeling that –

'You know what, Carter? I have a strange feeling that there's something about this murder scene … something that reminds me of something else.'

'It's not a film, is it? There have been lots of murder scenes in films. I've often –'

'No, it's not a film. Something in this murder scene makes me think of that other one – the one in Leyland.'

'You mean you think the murders were committed by the same person?'

'Almost certainly. I got that impression as soon as I entered the bedroom.' He looked around the room. 'We're missing something, Carter. You'll get yourself back in my good books if you can tell me what it is.'

Carter looked round the room. Carter looked very intently round the room. But Carter missed the size of the handkerchief and didn't even consider the ridiculous position of the calendar on the wall. So, naturally, he remained in Inspector Fullerton's bad books.

Chapter 14

Christmas Fun

Joan was upset. She was more upset now than she had ever been since realising she wasn't as pretty as other girls, or, in later life, as pretty as other women. She had heard from Melissa of her and Daphne's intention to share a flat. Joan had never been one for mixing after work with her colleagues at Fothergill's, but this was different. She couldn't help believing that since there had been so much animosity between the two for a couple of weeks, they had made up and decided to live together only because they were both pretty; they wouldn't have done it otherwise. Neither of them had ever suggested to her that they move into a flat together, even though she had never been on bad terms with either. It pointed to only one thing: how pretty they were.

She felt betrayed. She knew she was only a receptionist, and seldom saw Melissa except in the canteen, when she usually sat with her. Even so, they had both been at Fothergill's for far longer than Daphne, so why hadn't Melissa considered her as a flatmate? It wouldn't have hurt to ask. She might have been surprised by the answer, and wouldn't have needed to ask Daphne. But if that's how she felt, so be it. If she preferred Daphne's company to hers, what was the point in making herself ill by worrying about it? They were bound to start arguing again. It was only a matter of time before one of them moved out and the other wouldn't be able to afford the rent on her own. Serve her right.

Even as she thought this, she realised it was childish. What did it matter to her if Melissa and Daphne shared a flat together? She had her own life to live. She liked being on her own. She liked her job and was reasonably happy.

Except that she wasn't enjoying her job at the moment. She often felt miserable now, sitting at her desk with no one to talk to. It was always like that for girls and young women who weren't pretty;

men couldn't be bothered with them, unless they were ugly themselves. That annoyed her now more than it ever had. It was why no one ever tried to kiss her at the staff's annual Christmas party. That annoyed her now more than it ever had, even though this year the party hadn't been held yet; it was due the following afternoon. But no one *would* try to kiss her, she knew. Chester would as usual try to kiss Melissa, and she'd let him have one; and he'd probably try to kiss Daphne, and she'd probably let him. But if he tried to kiss her, she'd slap his face – as she would have done at previous Christmas parties, if he'd tried to do it then.

He didn't try to do it. He didn't even try to kiss Melissa or Daphne. He wasn't in the best of moods. Those curlers had humiliated him. Ever since then he'd been planning revenge. The Christmas party would have been the ideal time for it. For a while he had thought of suggesting – at the party – that because they had a 'resident expert' (referring to George, of course), they could hold a séance there and then. 'Who knows,' he would laugh, 'George might even call up the ghosts of Christmas past, present, and future, like those who visited Scrooge.' But he knew it wouldn't work. It was bound to sound weak after those damned curlers. Better no joke at all than a weak one. He would wait, he decided, till he came up with something devastating.

So Chester was comparatively quiet early on, contenting himself with quaffing drink after drink as he tried to keep up with Gregory, who had been invited, and who did try to kiss Melissa and Daphne, but not Joan – and not Alysse. Sometimes a prettier woman presents a more daunting challenge than one who isn't pretty at all.

Nor was he the only one to steal a kiss off the two prettiest women there. Two of the younger men from Mr Millar's production team seized the opportunity. One even gave it a go with Alysse, and got a sharp rebuke for his trouble; though neither of them, needless to say, even thought of approaching Joan.

There was music from somewhere, of the type that appealed to younger people, and there were plenty of paper hats being worn. Even Mr Fothergill wore one. 'It suits you,' laughed Alysse, contributing her one amusing remark to the festivities. 'Yes, I always look good in a paper hat,' responded Mr Fothergill. 'I'm thinking of wearing one all the time. It'll make a change from my bowler.'

Yes, he did actually wear a bowler as a rule. He had to take it off in his car; but walking back and to between the car park and his office, he always wore it.

But he didn't wear it when he made his customary Christmas speech, thanking all the members of staff for putting in such a stirling effort throughout the year – 'especially in respect of our *Two Puzzles and One Murder* series. That has been an enormous success.' Cheers from his audience. 'An unparalleled success,' he emphasised to more cheers. 'We have reached *No. 4* at the moment, and though it has been in the stores for only a couple of weeks, there are signs that it is selling well. You all did superbly to get it out before Christmas, and I can't praise you enough for that.' (More cheers.) 'What we have to do in the new year is prepare *No. 5*. We won't have to rush that. Sales are bound to drop during January; people are more interested in buying expensive sale items then. But once we have an idea what we want to do, I'm sure you'll do another fantastic job on what is required.' (More cheers.) 'I know Mr Dawes here will provide us with another excellent work of art.' (Cheers from Chester, who was still sitting next to Gregory.)

All that and more from Mr Fothergill in an orange paper hat.

The party went on and, as far as Gregory and Chester were concerned, so did the drinking. So much so that as people started to think about going home, Chester, in a slightly befuddled state, couldn't resist.

'I say, everyone,' he cried, struggling to his feet. 'I've got an idea. We could have a séance before we go.' His voice was rising and falling with the promise of a hiccup now and then. 'We have our very own Fothergill expert on séances. Take a bow, George.' He gestured to George to do as he bid, but George merely pressed his lips together grimly. 'He can – I have this on good authority – summon up the spirits. George, tell us what we should do to summon Christmas past. He can tell us what you did to that young woman on Christmas Eve that time.' This brought roars of laughter. 'And what you did to that young other woman the year before.' More roars of laughter. 'And what you did to that – Oh, no, I'd better not say. You can get into trouble for that sort of thing.' He touched the side of his nose a few times with a forefinger, indicating that he and George shared a secret. Whatever that was, if anything, there was more laughter.

George had been building up his courage. He could shoot Chester down in flames if he carried it off. His beaver joke.

''I say, Chester,' he called out above the merriment – 'what's that beaver doing on your head? Building a dam –'

If George had stopped there, as he should have done, he might have provoked some laughter at Chester's expense; a few people might have thought it funny. If only one person had, it would have been enough. But at that point, George's wires somehow got crossed; maybe he too had had more than his fair share. The 'dam' he spoke of must have sounded – sounded to himself – more like a swear word than an obstruction on a river; for he *didn't* stop there. He went on, after a hesitation, with 'thing', so what he said was: 'I say, Chester – what's that beaver doing on your head? Building a damn thing?' … which rather puzzled everyone, so that they fell silent. What damn thing? They quickly realised that he'd spoilt his own joke, so they sniggered at him, not at Chester. Since George didn't realise they were sniggering at him, and Chester hadn't heard what he was saying anyway, neither of them felt that he was the loser in that little confrontation; which was probably why it was the last anyone heard about séances or toupees from either of them.

*

Joan hadn't enjoyed herself at the party. She kept noticing how Melissa and Daphne were always chatting together, and resented it whenever either spoke to her; she didn't like being patronised. But she didn't make a scene. She took it all in her stride, as she was wont to do. She prided herself on her ability in that respect, and if she felt miserable – which she did – she wasn't about to make anyone else's Christmas party miserable as well. She would rise above it, for her own sake and the sake of others. Not that she made anyone else's Christmas party more enjoyable by doing so; no one seemed to notice. They went on enjoying themselves or not, as they would have done or not if she hadn't been there. She rose above that as well. If she wasn't being noticed, it was something to which she had long been accustomed.

When she went home later she was still feeling miserable and still rising above it.

But at least she didn't get arrested on the way.

Neither did Chester. He evaded the police traps. He had always been lucky in that respect; had never been convicted for speeding or drunken driving.

Gregory had, and he did get arrested on his way home. The police pulled him up as he drove partly in the wrong lane. The breathalyser did its trick and he was taken to the station, the inside of which did nothing to clear his mind, and in fact seemed to have an even more intoxicating effect on him. It made him chattier, and eager to demonstrate festive feelings towards his fellow man. He promised the arresting officer to paint his portrait free of charge as a gift for his mother, the offer of which brought a smile to the officer's face.

'You don't think I can paint your portrait?' slurred the scandalised Gregory. 'I'm an artist, my good man. I can paint the you-know-what off Jayne Mansfield.' The smile on the officer's face grew broader. 'And off your mother, if she'd like to pose for me.' The smile disappeared from the officer's face. 'What d'you say, officer,' – he was pawing the officer's shoulder now – 'would you and your mother like to pose for me?'

The officer made no reply. Likewise the desk sergeant when Gregory made a similar suggestion to him.

'Your moustache, sergeant – I'd like to paint it,' he said as he reached out to touch it.

The sergeant backed away and then locked him up.

He was released the following morning, so he wasn't obliged to spend Christmas Day behind bars. He had been charged and faced the threat of a ban, but at least his visit to the police station had given him an idea for a painting: a group of repulsive-looking policemen with sneering expressions as they put handcuffs on an old woman wearing a threadbare coat who had been caught shoplifting. He would call it 'The police triumph again'. He was full of it on his way home; couldn't wait to get started. But when he got home he poured himself a drink and never thought of it again.

Melissa went to two more parties over Christmas with her new boyfriend Richard, and for a laugh even went carol singing outside houses. Chester spent Christmas Day at his sister's, where he tried to amuse his little niece but failed, though she did keep staring at his toupee as though she thought that was funny. Daphne spent hers at home, where she had to keep pushing her little nephew's hand away when he tried again and again to touch one of her breasts, as though he thought they were funny. Alysse refused all invitations, preferring to keep the day free for herself to do as she wished without being subject to the foolish whims and stupid tastes of other people. George hoped he would get an invitation from someone but didn't. Joan refused to admit to herself that she wanted an invitation from someone, or that she was waiting for the phone to ring, or that she would have got dressed in a trice and dashed out before the person inviting her out had changed his mind. Mr Millar gave no indication that he knew Christmas had arrived, though somewhere beneath that lack of facial expression, there must have been some conscious acknowledgement of the fact.

Mr Fothergill enjoyed his Christmas, as he always did; Mrs Fothergill likewise. They should have been past the age when they bothered with presents. But of course they did. Mr Fothergill bought his wife a box of After Eight creams; Mrs Fothergill bought him a bottle of rather expensive white wine, to which he was partial at that time of year, as indeed she was. Better than either, however, was seeing their grandchildren again. And they didn't stint with the presents for them. Not only jigsaws either. Following advice from the children's parents – their own children – they'd bought them video games and various sporting items, such as a cricket bat for

Jamie and a pink tutu for Celestine, who, by coincidence, alas, had bought her grandmother a box of After Eight creams. The box Mr Fothergill had bought was quickly hidden away to avoid disappointing the girl.

Edgar Rice Root spent his Christmas – all of it, all week of it, right through to the New Year's Day – reading *Anna Karenina*.
    Reading and reading and reading *Anna Karenina*.

Chapter 15

Gathering Clues

Edgar's eyes were bloodshot as he stared down at the book he'd just closed. He looked drained of the spirit that had made him the murderer he was. And angry – he was very angry. He'd slogged his way through the whole damn thing and there hadn't been a mention of a pawnbroker. Or of a murder. There had been a suicide – Anna's; but what could that possibly have to do with the jigsaw? Nothing. And suicides were silly. Especially hers. Throwing herself under a train! What if she'd only lost her legs? How dumb would that be!

He pushed the book a few inches further away to show his disgust at everything to do with Anna Karenina. The jigsaw must relate to a different novel. Perhaps another thousand-pager! The thought frightened him. *Anna Karenina* wasn't a thousand pages long – it had seemed it but it wasn't. So there was no reason to assume that anything else by Tolstoy would be, even if *War and Peace* was. Well, he wasn't going to read anything else by Count Leo Tolstoy, so it didn't matter. He didn't care what the novel was, what the murder in the jigsaw was, or who committed it or ... He'd take *Anna Karenina* back to the library and he wouldn't even enquire about anything else the man had written. He'd dump it on the counter and walk straight out, and then he'd come home and dump the jigsaw in the bin, where it belonged.

That was his avowed intention; yet he didn't go and get the jigsaw and dump it in the bin there and then. Something held him back. But he did return the book. And he didn't enquire about other novels by Tolstoy. On the other hand, he didn't immediately leave the library. He drifted from shelf to shelf, running his eyes over the titles of the books. He had no intention of borrowing anything else but he had some time to spare.

He didn't make any move to look on the shelf containing classics, or on the shelves containing book by authors whose names began with a 'T'. And not finding anything that caught his interest particularly, he at last made for the exit … before turning round and heading for the shelf containing the classics and then to the shelf containing the 'T's.

There was nothing else by Tolstoy. So then he did leave the library, refusing absolutely to ask the assistant anything.

There was only one way to relieve his frustration, and a week later Inspector Fullerton was called in to investigate the murder of an old man in Fleetwood.

'It's the same murderer,' he asserted to Detective Sergeant Carter. 'I can feel it in my bones. Can't you, Carter?'

'I think I can, sir.'

'Think? Think, Carter? Don't think – feel it. That's the secret of being a good cop. Thinking too much can get you into all kinds of difficulty. Something you think can very easily be set against something else you can think, and there's no way of knowing which is more acceptable to reason. There's a place for it, I don't deny; but never reject what you instinctively feel. I instinctively feel that there's something about this murder scene which is almost exactly the same as the previous one. But what? That's what we need to find out. Clues – that's what we want. Keep looking, Carter. But make sure you distinguish what things are clues from what things aren't. That calendar on the wall, for instance. If you remember, there was one of those, exactly like it, on the wall of the bedroom where Mrs Godfrey was found dead. But that's just a coincidence. Lots of people have calendars on walls. There's no reason to think it's got anything to do with the murder. These things here, though,' – he was pointing to a silver ring on one chair and a feather on another – 'puzzle me. What the hell are they doing on chairs like this – as if they're just sitting there? In fact, they remind me of that dog. Remember – that fluffy dog at Mrs Shipley's? That was sitting on a chair the way they are. Is that a coincidence? A strange one if it is. Do you know what, Carter? I think we – you – should go back to that house and find out more about that dog. Ask the relatives. It might mean nothing, but you never know. It's too odd a coincidence for us to ignore it.'

So Carter got in touch with the deceased Mrs Shipley's son and daughter, neither of whom could tell him anything about the dog – except that they'd never seen it before, and couldn't understand why it was there in their mother's house. She'd never told them she'd bought a fluffy dog, and she wasn't a person who bought dolls of any kind. Carter asked them if they still had it. The daughter admitted that she'd taken it for her own daughter, who had got red paint on her hands while playing with it. The paint was dry, she explained, but because of the material it still left marks on her daughter's fingers. Carter asked if the police could borrow the dog as an aid to their investigations. The daughter agreed, and in no time Carter had picked it up and taken it in to show Inspector Fullerton.

They didn't have the man's handkerchief they'd missed as a clue – or any of the calendars – but they had brought to the station the feather and the silver ring and, of course, the club used as a murder weapon. To these was now added the fluffy doll dog. Fullerton spread them out on the table in his office. He looked at each one in turn.

'There's something about them,' he said. 'You know what, Carter – I have the feeling they were deliberately left where they were. Planted there so we would find them. Why else would they be there … sitting on chairs, as you or I might have been? Why? Why would that be? Come on, Carter – make suggestions. You are a detective, not a bus driver.'

Carter turned crimson. His father had been a bus driver, and Fullerton knew that. It wasn't right to cast aspersions about bus driving – because that's what he was doing, implying that bus drivers were too thick to think for themselves.

'I just feel there's something missing,' he ventured.

'Oh, you think that, do you? Of course there's something missing – our understanding! The solution to the mystery. We need to fit all the missing pieces together to solve the murder – the murders ... the barbaric acts that have left these old people dead. Good God, man – what are you smiling about?'

'Sorry sir. When you said "missing pieces", it made me think of a jigsaw. We bought Ryan, out little boy, a jigsaw for Christmas. *Two Puzzles and One Murder No. 3* it's called. We bought the first two and enjoyed them so much we got him the third as well. Have you not seen them in the shops?'

'I'm not in the business of buying jigsaws, Carter.'

'Oh, these are good fun, sir. You do the jigsaw, look for clues, and have to guess which murder in fiction is being depicted. My wife got the first one almost straight away – Bill Sikes' murder of that woman in *Oliver Twist*. She likes Charles Dickens, so she –'

'Yes, I'm sure it's all good fun, but we're to investigate a real-life murder, not a fictional one. So can we get back to the job at hand? This ring, for instance. You've seen the inscription, have you – "From R"? Was it a gift for the victim, and if so who gave it to her? Where was the inscription done? Who asked for it to be done? Why was it placed on the chair? If the murderer put it there, is he taunting us – challenging us to catch him? Lots of questions needing answers, Carter, about a real-life murder – *real-life* murder. You, it seems, are more interested in discussing jigsaws. Get a grip, man.'

Carter bristled. That wasn't fair, as far as he was concerned.

'I did point out the calendars, sir.'

'What calendars?'

'The calendars on the walls at the murder scenes. Didn't I think they were a clue?'

Fullerton was both indignant and contemptuous. 'No, you didn't. I pointed out the calendars and said they were a coincidence.'

'Oh!'

'Yes – Oh! You didn't mention the calendars at all. They weren't a clue: they were a coincidence. You have to learn to tell the difference. If you spend your time investigating coincidences, you might as well *be* a bus driver for what good you are to detective work.'

'There's nothing wrong with being a bus driver, sir.'

'Indeed there isn't – unless you have aspirations to be a top-notch detective. So show me, Carter, that you've got what it takes to be one. Come on – what's the link between all these clues? Solve the mystery for me.'

Carter looked down at the objects on the table and pulled his face.

'I still think there's something missing, sir.'

Fullerton snorted.

'A calendar perhaps? Maybe you think a calendar should be there. Is that the missing piece of the jigsaw? You numbskull, Carter.'

When he got home later, Carter complained to his wife Charlene, about how Fullerton treated him. She was plump in all the wrong places, but he thought her the prettiest woman in the world, even though she couldn't hold a candle to Melissa, whom, of course, he had never seen. Whether she was prettier than, or as pretty as, Daphne was debatable.

'He talks to me as though I'm an idiot. He actually called me a numbskull. It's not right, Charlie. If he was calling somebody else a numbskull – and if that person *was* a numbskull – it still wouldn't be right. It's humiliating. Demoralising. I can stand it because I've got you behind me. Other people wouldn't be able to. He could ruin a person's career by talking to him like that.'

'Just pay no attention to him, Adrian. You're a good detective – I know you are.' Every time Carter's wife addressed him by his first name, she wondered how she had ever come to marry a man named Adrian. She thought it such a funny name – a bit effeminate, which Carter wasn't. She was getting used to it, but it still caused a bit of a shiver.

'Oh, I ignore it. But he never stops. It's one thing after another. If I'm not a numbskull, I'm an idiot. If I'm not an idiot, I'm a clot. How would you like it if I kept on at you like that all the time.'

'I'd scratch your eyes out,' Charlene replied with a smile. 'Why not try that?'

Carter gave a curt, determined nod. 'Right – tomorrow. One more insult from Inspector Frederick Fullerton and he'll have no more eyes.'

'That's the spirit. Now go and help Ryan finish that jigsaw while I get the chicken ready.'

Chapter 16
An Unexpected Development

Mr Fothergill had every reason to feel pleased with the way business had gone during the previous twelve months. The *Two Puzzles and One Murder* series had been an unqualified success; sales had continued to grow and bonuses were duly and deservedly won. There wasn't one person employed at Fothergill's – including Chester – who didn't feel grateful for, or reap some benefit from, the consumers' continuing interest in the project. They were financially better off and, at the same time, felt a pride at being involved in giving innocent pleasure to thousands.

A pride in giving innocent pleasure.

That's what they felt.

Alas, not everyone thought they should feel it. Mr Fothergill received letters in January from two women who castigated the company – and so him as the head of that company – for, as one of them put it, 'pandering to the violent urges in all of us'. Mr Fothergill was astonished at that particular remark, never having experienced – as far as he could recall – any violent urges in his whole life. He recognised that other people had them, yes, but to say that he was pandering to them was going too far. Why, he'd deliberately rejected a series on real-life murders for that very reason. The fictional murders in his jigsaws were already on public sale in the novels and play in which they occurred; it wasn't as if he'd invented them. Since he never ignored the people who wrote to him, he replied to both women courteously, gently suggesting that perhaps they were being over-sensitive, a bit 'touchy'.

It wasn't wise to use a word like 'touchy' to women (whether they were pretty or not). And had he known the outrage it would engender he wouldn't have done so. If anything was bound to upset them, that particular word was. It suggests they are weak and emotional – a charge they are ever ready to fight to disprove. When they are also on a crusade to make the world a better place, the word seems to them to belittle their campaign and pour scorn on it. And that is unacceptable.

Consequently, the two women wrote – independently of each other – to their favourite newspapers, and expressed their discontent with the 'Murder series', as one of them deliberately called it, on various social media like Twitter. One of them, Stella King, was a writer of a blog, which she used to excoriate Fothergill Puzzles and the 'foolish gentleman' who had actually tried to defend 'his company's bloodthirsty attempt to gain profit from those who get a perverted thrill from anything to do with murder'.

This was to aim at other targets besides jigsaws, as Ms King went on to demonstrate, castigating filmmakers and novelists who 'spew the products of their sick minds on the gullible young in particular'.

Mr Fothergill never went on the internet to read blogs, and he didn't read this one, so he wasn't aware of how many people voiced support for her views. But many did. And as is always the case when instigators and followers encourage each other with a sense of moral activism, the campaign to destroy their opponents became a *raison d'etre* – a reason for living. Once it did, there was no saying to where it might lead.

One stop on the way was at the surgery of the Member of Parliament for the constituency in which Stella King lived. She called in there and spoke to Deidre Mullen, her MP, who had often spoken out against violence on television. She received a sympathetic hearing, although Mrs Mullen wouldn't support her in any effort to get the jigsaws banned.

'I find that a gentle approach is sometimes more likely to achieve a change in behaviour,' she boasted scandalously, never having given that impression to any of her colleagues in all the time she had been involved in politics. 'Keep writing to the gentleman you mentioned and stress the effect on the minds of the children who do the jigsaws. The more that the idea of murder enters their consciousness, the more likely it is to stay there; it becomes a way of thinking for them – murder instead of reasoned argument to get their own way. That's the way they'd start thinking. We know that children like to get their own way, and if they don't … well, sulking can very easily turn into thoughts of violent action to get it.'

Ms King agreed with the last part, though she wasn't sure that writing to 'that foolish gentleman' would achieve anything.

'He seems so fixed in his views – understandably, I suppose. He's a businessman who cares only about how much money he can make.'

'Oh, don't be so sure,' Mrs Mullen cautioned. 'Some businessmen do have consciences. He may need reminding of the fact, that's all.'

So Ms King wrote to Mr Fothergill again, reminding him of the fact, if he had forgotten it, that children are everyone's concern and we – he – should express that concern in the way we behave towards them. Giving them jigsaws about murder, she declared, was like handing them a loaded gun or a knife. So shame on him for doing so!

Mr Fothergill was having none of that. When he showed the letter to his wife, he spluttered with indignation.

'The cheek of it! Shame on me for giving them jigsaws to do – have you ever heard such nonsense?'

'I don't think she's saying that exactly, dear,' Mrs Fothergill replied soothingly. 'But you're right, of course. Think of all the gruesome fairy tales children read; they're horror stories, some of them. And thousands of children have read *Oliver Twist*, or seen the film. Heavens! They can see that on television most Christmases.'

That was a point Mr Fothergill made when he wrote back to Ms King a few days later, after calming down and giving a lot of thought to what he would say; he didn't want to receive any more letters from her, and hoped this one would put an end to their correspondence. He didn't use the word 'touchy' again but did suggest that she was, perhaps, being a bit more protective of children than was, perhaps, good for them. 'You wouldn't want to stop them reading Grimm's fairy tales, would you?' he asked as a parting shot.

He meant it rhetorically. And she read it as he meant it. But that didn't stop her answering it – because a couple of days later another letter from Ms King arrived.

'Yes, I would! I would want to stop them reading Grimm's fairy tales. And I do!! I have a little girl of my own and I wouldn't dream of subjecting her to the horrors contained in them. Do you really think a child can read such stuff and not be affected by it? Or can't you see what's happening in the world, to the people who live in it? Have you no interest in the well-being and sanity of our children? Do you not realise how disturbed many of them are because of the vicious and malignant culture we have created for our sick pleasures?'

Mr Fothergill had to look away from the letter for a moment. What an extraordinary tirade! She could write, though, he had to admit; she had an effective turn of phrase. He read on.

'I urge you now, before you do any more damage to our youngsters, to withdraw your jigsaws from sale and cease their production.'

The last part made him chuckle. It was just so ridiculous. Who did this woman think she was? Then his face grew grim. The best thing this time would be to ignore her; he couldn't spend his time answering letters as rude as this one. How dare she suggest that he had no interest in the well-being of children – or in their sanity! How preposterous! Some people get so worked up over things they feel strongly about; they lose all sense of proportion.

He decided to call a staff meeting and let everyone else at Fothergill's know that they were literally under attack. Until then he had kept the letters to himself, seeing no reason to upset anyone involved in the production of the jigsaws. Some of the women especially, he assumed ...

In fact, when he told them, they were less upset than amused. Melissa opened her mouth in surprise, which caused Daphne to do likewise, confirming that the two of them were still on course for sharing a flat; and caused Joan also to do likewise, confirming that she would have been happy to share a flat with either, had she only be asked. Alysse gave a toss of her head, either to show that she wouldn't have shared a flat with any of them even if she had been asked, or to convey her even greater contempt for the complaint than Mr Fothergill had.

Chester suggested sending Ms King a complimentary jigsaw.

'We could tell her to let her daughter do the jigsaw and then see how it affects her over the years. If she turns out to be a murderer, then fine; we'll agree to do what she wants and withdraw the jigsaws from sale.'

Even George smiled at this. Mr Millar didn't, though that isn't to say he didn't find it funny. Melissa's shoulders shook as she chuckled, which caused Daphne's to do likewise; and caused Joan's almost to do likewise but not quite, since for some reason she had started to feel depressed. And for the rest of the meeting Joan paid little attention to what was being said or shared in the laughter directed at Ms King.

For this was more than the common depression brought on by a realisation that one isn't as pretty as other girls or other women. This went deeper. It sank, plummeted, to a gut feeling that she was rather sympathetic to Ms King's cause and wanted her to triumph against all the forces that Fothergill Puzzles could pit against her.

Of course, she wouldn't have put it like that, but there it all was in what might otherwise be described as a 'thirst for revenge' – first and foremost against Melissa and Daphne, but also against anyone who could be associated with them.

Not that she would ever have done anything, had revenge of a minor form not presented itself to her the very next day. That it did gave her an opportunity she eagerly accepted. She heard on local radio an interview of Ms King by a journalist, Jason Cawley, who introduced her as a campaigner against the increased use of violence in children's jigsaws. Joan felt that Mr Fothergill, who she assumed wouldn't have been listening to that particular programme, ought to know about it, so, waiting till Melissa was bound to be at her desk, she went up to inform him.

'I need to speak to Mr Fothergill at once,' she told Melissa in a tone of voice stressing the urgency of her request.

'What is it?' Melissa asked, immediately concerned. She could see how desperate Joan was.

'Is he in?' Joan pointedly ignored Melissa's question.

'Yes. What's the matter?'

'There's no one with him, is there?'

'No, but –'

Joan swept past her and walked straight in, unannounced, to Mr Fothergill's office.

Melissa's mouth dropped open, confirming that she hadn't a clue what the problem was.

Mr Fothergill knew nothing of the interview. When he heard from Joan what Ms King had been saying, the colour faded from his cheeks. As an elderly gentleman, he still thought of the radio as being more of a public platform than the internet, so learning that Ms King had been giving voice to her complaint over the airwaves disturbed him more than her blog would have done.

'Did she mention me?' he asked.

'Not by name, though she did keep calling you a "foolish gentleman".'

'Oh, did she?'

'She did.'

Mr Fothergill steeled himself against any delayed reaction to the insult. He'd been called foolish before on a number of occasions, going back to his schooldays, but it wasn't very nice to hear it, even from a foolish woman.

'And did she mention Fothergill Puzzles specifically?'

'She did, yes.'

'Hmm, this is more serious than I thought. Thank you for letting me know, Miss … er … Thank you.'

Joan forgave him for forgetting her second name; he was obviously distracted by what she'd told him. But she still hadn't forgiven Melissa. Passing her desk on the way out, she didn't even look at her,

'What is it?' Melissa asked again, her curiosity greater than ever.

Joan crossed to the door, and didn't look back even when Melissa cried out again: 'What's the matter, Joan?'

A minor form of revenge, but a satisfying one.

Joan decided not to eat in the canteen that day. She went instead to a nearby sandwich bar and had lunch alone, deriving whatever enjoyment she got from doing so. The longer Melissa was kept in ignorance of the radio interview, the more she would like it. She admitted that to herself as she sat there, munching on her chicken salad with mayonnaise. Yes, she was petty, she admitted that as well. She was a sad person who could be nasty in certain circumstances – that as well. Even so, she was smiling as she wiped a crumb from her lips. She was content.

In fact, she had got to Mr Fothergill just in time. For that very afternoon he received a phone call from the journalist who had interviewed Ms King, and who now wanted a response from him. Mr Fothergill wasn't accustomed to talking to the press, and floundered a bit in the face of Cawley's forceful questioning; but he made it clear that he rejected Ms King's criticisms and thought she was a bit of 'busybody'. That was the very word he used.

Unfortunately.

Chapter 17

Attacked on the BBC

Inspector Fullerton watched as Detective Sergeant Carter entered the room and nodded to him in greeting. He didn't nod back. He was in a bad mood. He had made no progress in his investigations of the murders on his patch and it bothered him. There had been no identification of anyone who was a serious suspect and the clues they had seemed more of a hindrance than a help. He felt like taking it out on Carter, so he did.

'Solved the murder yet, Carter?'

'Er … '

'The third one, wasn't it? You said you'd bought your little boy another jigsaw.'

'Oh, that one. Well, actually we did the jigsaw last night. My wife thinks it may be from an Agatha Christie novel, since it seems to be set in a country house. But she's not sure which one. She hasn't read any of her novels apart from –'

'Carter,' Fullerton interrupted him – 'look at me. Study my face carefully – my eyes, my expression. Can you see any intimation on it of any interest I might have in your jigsaw? Look closely. Focus on any aspect of it that might lead you to believe I'm grateful to be told that it might be a murder in an Agatha Christie novel. Funnily enough, Carter, I've read one or two novels by her in my time. I suggest *The Murder of Roger Ackroyd* might provide the answer; it often does when people are asked questions about her work. But jigsaws, Carter, are not really what we in our division of the police force are about. What we are about, Carter, are real-life murders, and we still haven't solved those we are currently investigating; so do me a favour and turn your mind to those. Forget your jigsaws for one day, if you can, and put the pieces together, if you can, of our own murder mysteries.'

Having arrived at the office with renewed enthusiasm for his job, Carter had almost immediately felt it wane as Fullerton began his diatribe; but the inspector's mention of his familiarity with the works of Agatha Christie, sparked his interest.

'Did you say *The Murder of Roger Ackroyd*, sir?'

'I did.'

'I wonder if that is the solution. There –'

'Don't try my patience, Carter. I have no intention of discussing children's jigsaws with you ever again. Speak to your little boy about them, if you must, but understand that I am a grown man who tries to do the job he is paid to do.' He turned towards the table. 'You haven't forgotten these things, have you?'

'No, sir.'

'Have you considered what they tell us?'

'Frankly, I'm not sure they tell us anything.'

'That's what you think, is it – that you don't think they tell us – you, repeat, you – anything? Well, let me tell you, Carter, that I think they tell us – me, repeat, me – a lot. They tell me that the murderer is not only a cunning, devious man, but a man with a sense of humour. He's having a bit of fun at our expense. He's challenging us to figure out what these clues mean. If we can find out what that is, what their significance is, we'll go a long way to capturing him.

He doesn't think we will. That's why he's getting cocky. That's why he's also stupid. That's why he's liable to make mistakes. That's why I have the feeling he's already made a mistake, if we could only see it. What is it, Carter? What's the mistake he's made?'

'If he has made one, sir. We don't know for –'

'Carter – do me a favour. Go back outside, and come back in as a very different person. Be somebody else with another name and no little boy you buy jigsaws for.'

'Well, we don't know. Everything he's done may have been thoroughly worked out and –'

'Carter – let's imagine he's made a mistake and we want to discover what it is. Any ideas?'

Carter studied the objects on the table – the fluffy doll dog, the chicken feather, the silver ring with the inscription, the club – and stroked his chin pensively.

'There's something very familiar about them,' he murmured.

'Yes, Carter, that isn't surprising. You saw them yesterday.'

'No, more than that. Something *very* familiar. That dog, for instance. I get the feeling I've seen one like that before.'

'Where, Carter – running round the park? In a pet shop?'

'To be honest, I'm not sure. Not a pet shop. I don't think I've ever been in a pet shop; but I'd be a liar if I said it couldn't be in a park. It could be but I don't think it is.'

Fullerton regarded him with disdain. 'Carter – are we any nearer to the solution to this mystery than we were when you entered the room?'

'I am trying, sir, but – well, have you any ideas?'

Fullerton's face darkened. He turned away. The truth was, he hadn't.

He looked at the objects on the table again.

'It's all there, Carter. The solution is there, if we can only see it.'

'Yes, sir, I agree…. But I still think there's something missing.'

Mr Fullerton hadn't realised that Jason Cawley was recording his remarks over the phone, and he didn't hear them when they were broadcast as his response to Ms King's attack. So he couldn't have known they were edited for brevity's sake, or that the word 'busybody' was left in.

Ms King heard it, was outraged, and discussed the matter with Deirdre Mullen, who, she insisted, was being called a busybody just as much as she was. The MP accepted this, was outraged, and broached the subject during a television interview. The interviewer was Carol Stoddard, who hadn't intended to raise the subject of violence in society but who knew that Mullen was an obsessive about it and would probably raise it herself – as indeed she did. Stoddard tried to divert her away, but in vain. Mullen ranted about being called a 'busybody'. No, she admitted, it wasn't her that the 'foolish gentleman' had called a busybody, but he was obviously referring to all those women who objected to how people like him made their fortunes, and she was one of those. And she didn't apologise for it. People should care how fortunes were made. They shouldn't be made by inflicting on children more and more vicious acts of thuggery. 'If that's what our children come to regard as perfectly normal, why should we expect them ever to behave differently themselves?' she demanded of Stoddard, as if the interviewer profoundly disagreed. 'Only jigsaws, you say; but that's to miss the point. It's the very fact that they are only jigsaws that I find most worrying. If we can see murder in things like jigsaws, it shows how far we've sunk in our quest for what some of us would regard as a civilised way of living.'

That was really piling it on; but the words 'murder in things like jigsaws' struck a chord with some viewers, including George. He was the one member of staff at Fothergill's who saw the interview. And he understood how damaging to the company such a remark could be. The following morning he hurried to Mr Fothergill's office to inform him of it.

'Is Mr Fothergill in?' he asked Melissa.

'He is, yes.'

'I need to speak to him at once.'

'Why – what on earth's the matter?'

'There's no one with him, is there?'

'No.'

George raised a finger as if to say 'I'll go in, then' and strode past her. He knocked on Mr Fothergill's door but didn't wait for an answer; he twisted the handle and walked in.

Mr Fothergill was aghast at what George told him. On the television! A Member of Parliament objecting to being a called a busybody – by him? He hadn't called *her* a busybody; he'd called that other woman one. But thousands of people – hundreds of thousands – would have heard her say it. Perhaps millions! And most of them would have believed her: it was on the television so it was bound to be true. Mr Fothergill didn't need to be told by George how damaging to his business that might be. He rather wished now he had agreed to a broadcast interview. He could have put his side of the argument in a less aggressive-sounding way. It probably did sound aggressive to use a word like 'busybody', especially to those he was using it against. But no, surely not, he told George.

'She's just complaining about it as a way of sounding more reasonable than I may have done. You know what politicians are like. They twist things all the time to suit their position.'

George agreed, but insisted it 'could still spell trouble'. He left Mr Fothergill to ponder that warning, with a nod of the head to show how seriously he viewed it.

Then he walked past Melissa with a tight-lipped expression on his face.

'What's the matter?' she asked, sensing that once again something she knew nothing about was causing concern.

George looked towards her as he opened the door to leave, then shook his head to show that, yes, there was something causing concern. But he didn't say what.

And the way he had looked at her and had shaken his head gave Melissa the erroneous impression that it might be something *she* had done, something silly or careless. She wondered what it might be. Her heart started beating more rapidly as she fretted over it. But then Mr Fothergill called her in and asked her if she had seen the interview. When he told her about it, her mouth dropped open to show how seriously she too regarded it. If Daphne had been present, her mouth would have followed suit, as it did later in the canteen when Melissa informed her about it. Nobody told Joan about it, so her mouth remained resolutely shut till she found out quite by chance a few days later from the postman, when her mouth opened very slowly, but without creaking as it didn't have any hinges.

Needless to say, Mrs Fothergill's mouth dropped open when Mr Fothergill told her about it, confirming that she had always hoped Fothergill Puzzles would one day get a mention on television. She didn't seem too upset by it.

'All publicity is good publicity,' she remarked to her husband's surprise.

'Really, Vera – you astonish me. I've been attacked on the BBC – I think it was the BBC – and you think it good for the company.'

'It is. Most people will agree with you that she is a busybody – making such a fuss over jigsaws. And whether they do or they don't, they'll want to see what the furore's about. It'll mean more and more people buying them.'

'That's not the point. I've always prided myself on providing puzzles that people enjoy doing. I don't want them to think there's anything nasty in what we're producing. These women are giving that impression.'

Then you need to go on television yourself to counter their arguments.'

'What – me? I'm not going on television. Not that I've been asked to do so, but I wouldn't anyway.'

'Why ever not?'

'Well … it's not something I'd want to do.'

'It'd be good publicity.'

'There you are again – talking about publicity, as if that's the only thing that matters. It isn't.'

'Well, the least you could do is write to the *Radio Times* and make your objections known to what that MP said.'

Mr Fothergill considered this.

'I think I will…. Yes, I will. I'd rather do that.'

The following week, Mr Fothergill's letter duly appeared in the *Radio Times*. He avoided any use of the words 'touchy' and 'busybody', but he did suggest that some women lose all sense when they're upset about something.

That was rather silly.

It was tantamount to declaring war.

Meanwhile, Edgar Rice Root had ordered *Resurrection* from the library. He had made enquiries about other novels by Tolstoy after all. Once he heard the title *Resurrection* it made him think of someone who had died – been murdered – and then been born again. It seemed a daft story, if that's what happened, but if a murder took place in it, he might find it was the very one he was looking for. So yes, in desperation he ordered a copy.

He didn't know what to expect but he feared another very long novel; writers of that era never knew when to stop. He'd come to understand that. What he hadn't yet come face to face with was a very long novel in small print. The copy that arrived for him *was* in small print. Despair coursed through him as he flicked through the pages when he went to pick it up. He looked at the assistant, who smiled at him, as if she knew – he thought – what an ordeal lay ahead for him, as if she was laughing at him because of it. He could have throttled her there and then. Instead, he gave every indication that this was precisely the copy he had hoped to receive – not fooling her for a moment – and then took the book home.

He started reading it straight away.

Two days later he had reached page 5 – and his eyes were sore.

Chapter 18

Agreement Reached

When word got round at Fothergill's that their employer had written a letter to the *Radio Times* in defence of his company's products, most of the people there hurried out to buy the magazine. Those who didn't were shown the letter by those who did; but whether they did or they didn't, there was unanimous approval for Mr Fothergill's response. Even the women temporarily abandoned their instinctive reaction to being told what 'some women' were like, while remaining indignant at Deirdre Mullen's lambasting of their jigsaws. Alysse had to make a considerable effort in that respect but she managed it.

George congratulated Mr Fothergill without in any way sounding obsequious.

'Well done, Mr Fothergill. I think you made your case extremely well. I'm sure the readers will be left in no doubt about the entertainment value of our jigsaws. They must see murders on television every night in one form or another. It's a pity you didn't make a list of all those programmes in which they occur; you could have filled two columns.'

Chester tried to get three cheers going, but the first 'Hip hip hooray' was as far as it went, as only George and Melissa were with him at the time and neither of them bothered to join in.

Even so, Mr Fothergill thanked them for supporting him.

'It makes a difference, you know, to realise you have your people behind you. I would hate to be fighting the good fight completely alone – especially against a Member of Parliament who is used to arguing her corner. That's not something I have to do very often.'

He couldn't have imagined that soon afterwards he would be doing it under intense public scrutiny.

On television.

For the following day he got a phone call from a producer at the BBC inviting him to a live broadcast discussion with Stella King on violence in jigsaws. It was the last thing he had expected or had wanted. His first inclination was to refuse.

'It's not something I'm used to doing,' he explained to the producer, Alan Nevinson.

'People might think you're ashamed,' insinuated Nevinson, whose persuasive powers were well known at the BBC.

'Ashamed? Of what?'

'Of encouraging children to spend their time engaged in violent pastimes.'

'Nonsense.'

'I agree – it is nonsense. But that's what some people will assume. And think of the damage it could do to your business if that belief spreads.'

Mr Fothergill was ready to dismiss that as poppycock; but then he remembered that George had said the same thing. He fell silent, allowing Nevinson to continue.

'Far better if you confront this … who is it? … Stella King, and put her in her place.'

Mr Fothergill liked the idea of that, but he still hesitated. It was something he decided he'd like to talk over with his wife.

'Yes, by all means,' Nevinson agreed. 'I'll ring you tomorrow. But believe me, Mr Fothergill, it's always best to clear the air over something like this. You may think it'll go away, but these days, with all the social media we have, I can assure you it won't. People will go on talking about it and, if you don't stand up for yourself, someone will slag you off for what you've done and persuade others that they're right and you're wrong. Before you know it, your name is mud.'

That was what Mr Fothergill told his wife when he got home.

'My name could be mud, according to him.'

Since Mrs Fothergill liked the idea of having her husband on the television even more than she liked the idea of having the name of Fothergill Puzzles on it, she voiced support for that view.

'It will be unless you let people know your side of the argument. I don't know what you've got to be frightened of –'

'Who's frightened? It's not a case of being frightened. I'm more than happy to stand up for myself. It's just that … on television … I'm not used to that.'

'There's a first time for everything. You'll be fine. You're making jigsaws, for heaven's sake, not toy guns that shoot plastic bullets. They're dangerous; jigsaws aren't.'

That was true. Mr Fothergill realised how true that was. He could use that during any discussion he eventually agreed to have. He could – he thought – list all the toys and games that were a hundred times more dangerous than the jigsaws he made. Even before he replied to his wife, he was searching in his mind for other things – like toy tanks and … why, yes, even water pistols. Yes, water pistols. They could knock a child's eye out if the jet of water shot into it powerfully enough.

'And water pistols,' he said. It had slipped his mind that what Stella King and Deirdre Mullen were objecting to was murder. Had water pistols been depicted in the jigsaws, they probably wouldn't have turned a hair. No matter. Mr Fothergill had made up his mind, or Mrs Fothergill had made it up for him, even if he didn't know it yet in either case. He couldn't let his company's name be traduced, or allow the sales of his jigsaws to tumble just because a silly woman or two didn't like the pictures. Yes, he would take part in a discussion with Stella King and put her in her place. He owed it to his employees. He wouldn't just be defending himself or his jigsaws; he'd be defending them as well.

He didn't say as much to any of them the following morning at work; it would have sounded too much like boasting. But he did tell Melissa and George that he would be appearing on television once arrangements had been made. Melissa's mouth dropped open, confirming once again how pretty she was, as she did have very nice white teeth. She was even more excited about the news than Mrs Fothergill, having always wanted to be on television herself. It was the height of celebrity for her. Even George was impressed, while maintaining a dignified restraint. He told Alysse, who didn't exactly groan but gave every indication that she would have done, had she been given a nudge in the back. Television meant nothing to her, and anyone appearing on it she regarded with suspicion, failing to understand why anyone would *want* to appear on it. Melissa told everyone else except Joan. That wasn't a deliberate omission on her part; it was simply that their paths didn't cross before Joan found out from Chester. But to have tried to persuade Joan that it wasn't deliberate would have been like trying to do a Fothergill jigsaw blindfolded.

When Alan Nevinson phoned again he was delighted to hear that Mr Fothergill was willing to participate in the broadcast. He offered to send a car to pick him up on the Friday – an offer turned down – and gave him some advance warning about what to expect before the programme went on air. Make-up – he would have to go to make-up. Mr Fothergill must have been aware of the necessity for that, but he still expressed surprise; and he later made a point of telling his wife that he would have to wear make-up.

'Of course, you will,' she laughed. 'All television stars have to do that. Just like film stars when they're making films.'

'I'm hardly a television star – or ever will be,' Mr Fothergill protested. 'I've never worn make-up in my life.' He sounded wonderstruck.

'I should jolly well hope not. Otherwise I'd begin to doubt the man I married all those years ago.'

Edgar Rice Root had made progress. Slow progress. He couldn't read any faster than he was doing; his eyes wouldn't let him. Every now and then his vision grew fuzzy around the perimeter of what they could take in and made more and more words on the page blurry and illegible. He had to keep turning his eyes away or even closing them for a while. The fear struck him that he would have to start wearing glasses – something he had never had to do or had ever wanted to do. He also wondered whether he'd be able to get to the end of the novel; to do so was hardly worth the bother of ruining his eyesight. And yet before long there was, apparently, a poisoning – a murder by a prostitute of one of her clients. A poisoning wasn't an axe killing, and it wasn't administered in a pawnbroker's, but it was a start. Maybe there were more murders to come. He could go blind; he knew he could go blind but he read on….

Inspector Fullerton had been checking the dates of all the unsolved murders in his area, looking for a pattern. He couldn't find one. He hadn't seen the link between those committed on the date of a full moon and those that weren't committed on such a date but did have one ringed on a calendar pinned to a wall overlooking the dead body. It didn't matter much; for Fullerton had little doubt that all of them had been committed by the same man. Little doubt, but no evidence to point the finger at any particular suspect. What was he missing? That was a question that haunted him morning, noon and night, even when he wasn't investigating anything; it was a habit – but a good one for a man with his job, he liked to think, so he didn't mind. In this case it was relevant anyway: he *was* missing something.

And here was the man to tell him what it was, he joked to himself as Carter entered the room. He pushed his chair back onto its two rear legs, leaned back with exaggerated repose, and noticed that Carter had broken out into a broad grin. What was all that about? Not that he really wanted to know.

'You were right, sir,' said Carter.

Fullerton didn't ask for clarification, so Carter told him.

'That jigsaw. It was the murder in *The Murder of Roger Ackroyd*. My wife read it over the weekend, and it all matched. All the clues in the jigsaw were there in the book – even the goose quill. It was awfully well done.'

Fullerton gazed at him, wondering whether to explode or to say something sarcastic.

'So I solved that murder, did I, Carter?'

'You did, sir. Congratulations.'

'Thank you, Carter. You're congratulating me for solving a murder in a jigsaw, are you?'

'Yes, sir. But the funny thing is –'

'No, Carter – there is nothing funny about it. I worked hard at solving the mystery of the murder in the jigsaw, and –'

'No, sir, I'm not saying that –'

'Oh, I could have sworn you said "the funny thing is".'

'Yes, sir, the funny thing is that one of the clues we spotted was a ring.'

'A ring? What's funny about that?'

'Nothing. There's nothing about the ring *per se*.'

'Carter, if there's one thing I hate more than anything, it's the use of foreign words and phrases to say something that could equally be said in English. Haven't we had this conversation before about Americanisms?'

'I, er …. Don't think so, sir. Perhaps it was somebody –'

'No, by God, it was you. I can't recall the exact Americanism you used, but any one of a million would have been enough to annoy me. So cut out the *per se* gobbledegook and say what you have to say – in English.'

'Yes, sir. Well, I was saying there was nothing wrong with the ring itself … as a ring –'

'Thank you.'

'What was funny about it – a coincidence, if ever there was one, if you ask me – was that the ring had an inscription on it.' Here Carter waited for Fullerton to ask him what the inscription was. Fullerton didn't, so Carter told him anyway. 'The inscription being "From R".' Now he waited for Fullerton to show some surprise. Fullerton didn't, so Carter repeated the inscription. '"From R" – isn't that amazing?'

Fullerton continued to stare at him.

'Isn't what amazing?'

'"From R" – like the ring we found at the murder scene.'

Fullerton at last showed some appreciation of what seemed to be a genuine coincidence.

'It is amazing, yes; I admit it. A curious coincidence. Very odd. You'll have to write a book sometime about amazing coincidences in your line of work. I'm sure it'll be a best seller. Is that all you have to report – the latest in your attempt to solve the murders in the jigsaws?'

Carter started chuckling.

'Well, actually sir, you're not going to believe this. There is something else. Another coincidence. Hard to credit, really, but I swear it's true.'

'I'm waiting, Carter. Please get to the point.'

'Well ... my little boy did the *No. 1* jigsaw again last night; I'd forgotten all about it till I saw the picture again. Do you remember that time I said there was something about that fluffy dog – the one we found at one of the murder scenes – which reminded me of something?' Carter waited for Fullerton's response. Fullerton didn't respond, so Carter told him anyway. 'Well, there was a dog in the jigsaw ... a dog with red legs, just like the one we found. How about that for a coincidence? Incredible, I'd say. That's two, I reckon, for my book.'

Fullerton was still staring at Carter, but now with a different expression. He lowered the chair till it was on its four legs again and peered up at Carter.

'A dog with red legs in one jigsaw, and a ring with the inscription "From R" in another? That is odd. Very odd.'

'That's what I thought, sir.'

'Did you see anything else in the jigsaws which reminded you of anything?'

'How do you mean, sir?'

'How do I mean? What kind of talk is that, Carter? Don't you mean "What do you mean?" Doesn't "What" make more sense than "How" in that context?'

'Sorry, sir.'

'Carter – what I want you to do is to go home and bring back all your jigsaws.'

'All my jigsaws, sir?

'Yes, Carter. Go now and bring them straight away.'

Carter looked puzzled and took about ten seconds before he moved from where he was standing; but he went eventually – only too happy that his little boy was at school. He was a bit of a cry baby and, if he'd seen his father taking his jigsaws away, he would have bawled his head off. Carter, for his part, hated to see his little boy in tears and would have been thrown into turmoil at his distress.

As it was, he returned to the station within an hour, carrying all four of the *Two Puzzles and One Murder* jigsaws.

'Good, Carter,' said Fullerton. 'I had a terrible feeling that when I told you to bring all your jigsaws you might bring a dozen or more.'

'No, sir; there are only four of these. I didn't think you'd want the one with bunny rabbits on it,' Carter grinned.

'Good thinking, Carter.'

'And my wife agreed, so I left that one at home.'

'Yes, it's always nice to have a woman to help with the difficult decisions. Wouldn't you say so?' Fullerton was inspecting the outsides of the boxes.

'I would. My wife –'

'Right, Carter, let's get down to business. You say there was, what, a dog with red legs in the first jigsaw?'

'Yes, sir.'

'And a ring with the inscription "From R" in which?'

'The third, sir.'

'Right. We'll do the second one.'

'Sir?'

'We'll do the second one. Clear some of that stuff from the table.

'We're doing the jigsaw?'

'Well, there are no pictures on the boxes, so we'll have to, won't we? And seeing as you're so used to doing them, I'll bow to your greater experience. I'll watch till I know how it's done. Get cracking.'

Chapter 19

The Debate

Mrs Fothergill accompanied Mr Fothergill to the television studio. They were both dressed to the nines. Mr Fothergill was wearing a black suit and waistcoat under a black overcoat, Mrs Fothergill a cream-coloured knee-length coat. There had been a light fall of snow and their feet crunched through it as they walked toward the entrance to the building.

'You won't see anyone here who's in *Coronation Street*,' he told her. 'This is the BBC, not ITV.'

'I'm well aware of that,' Mrs Fothergill replied in a tone conveying the pride she felt at being a self-proclaimed expert on the programme.

They entered the building and Mr Fothergill gave his name at the reception desk. Shortly afterwards a young woman came to escort him to where he had to go. She was prettier than Joan, but that was the best one could say of her. She introduced him to Alan Nevinson, a lean, oval faced man with a prominent Adam's apple who immediately complimented Mr Fothergill on his smell. It was true. Mr Fothergill had slapped on some after-shave lotion. It was something he seldom did. But he was able to tell Mr Nevinson what it was called, and felt more at ease for doing so. Until then he had been apprehensive. It was an example of unintended consequences – though in this case for the better.

Nevinson also made a fuss of Mrs Fothergill, his eyes flitting all over her person as he sought for something to praise. Finding nothing, he merely smiled at her from time to time and once even clasped his hands towards her, as if that said everything he would have liked to say but hadn't found anything to justify it.

He was giving them a rundown on the pre-programme procedures when a ginger-haired man in a brown sports jacket and orange tie joined them. It was Don Clement, who would be hosting the debate. More smiles and handshakes followed and calming words were expressed. Mr Fothergill wondered whether he would meet his adversary before they confronted each other before the camera.

'Yes, we'll introduce you. She's in make-up at present, and that's where you should go now.' Saying which, he placed his right arm round Mr Fothergill's back – without touching him – and pointed the way with his left.

Alysse knew she would be watching the programme; but that didn't stop her wondering whether she should, or wanted to, or could be bothered to, or would find it more convenient to forget. Well, she couldn't do the last of these, as she was now sitting in front of her television waiting for it to start.

Chester was in front of his and he *couldn't wait* for it to start. He was lounging back in his armchair with a drink to hand, as he usually was before the start of the FA Cup Final. He was there to shout encouragement to Mr Fothergill, as he would have done to the team he supported – Brentford – if it had ever got to the Final. He did support Mr Fothergill and was raring to go with 'Boo's and hisses against his opponent as and when required.

George was watching with a more serious demeanour, intending to view the imminent confrontation in as fair-balanced a way as he could.

Melissa wouldn't have missed it for the world, and even refused to go to the pictures with her new boyfriend Duncan so she could stay at home and watch it with her mother, as did Daphne. The two were so alike in some respects that it wasn't surprising that they were planning to share a flat. But the difference in their reactions once Mr Fothergill's rubicund features appeared on the screen suggested future difficulties in their relationship.

Daphne nudged her mother to confirm that the face did indeed belong to her employer.

Melissa squealed, and cried: 'That's him! That's Mr Fothergill!'

What they all saw on the screen was a nervous-looking Mr Fothergill doing his best to stop his face from twitching. Don Clement – 'I like him,' Melissa told her mother – was introducing him to the viewers. Mr Fothergill said 'Thank you' when he should have said 'Hello', though he should have said neither with the sickly smile he displayed. Clement then turned to Stella King and explained to the viewers that she was the person who had made the initial complaints about the jigsaws – which he did in a sceptical tone, suggesting that he was very much on Mr Fothergill's side.

That didn't matter at all. Stella King needed no one on her side. She was dark-haired woman in her thirties, with a severe expression that may have been a daily phenomenon on her features or may have been specially cultivated for the occasion. Whether she was pretty or not wasn't something one thought of asking about Ms King. She was what she was – beyond prettiness and any other demeaning description.

Clement opened the discussion with what appeared to be a helpful opening for Mr Fothergill.

'Clearly, Mr Fothergill, you weren't trying to incite children to violence with your jigsaws?'

It wasn't a difficult question, but Mr Fothergill, still conscious of the hot lights shining down on him and the technicians gathered round, took some seconds to respond. But eventually:

'Good heavens, no. Our jigsaws are made so that the people who buy them can have some fun putting them together. It's as simple as that…. And, I might add, there's also an educational aspect to these particular jigsaws. We thought it a way of bringing great works of fiction to people of all ages, not just the young –'

'Bringing murder to people of all ages, you mean,' Ms King broke in.

'Well, that is a consequence of depicting the murders in the jigsaws,' agreed Mr Fothergill, who had surprised himself by how quick his response was; 'but the murders are already there in the great works of fiction. If you're going to criticise me or my company for producing these jigsaws, you should also criticise the likes of Charles Dickens for describing murders in his novels.' Mr Fothergill had rehearsed this argument many times since agreeing to the debate, and he felt a sense of triumph at now having made it. (He wasn't to know that when he did, Chester raised a fist in the air and shouted 'Yes!')

'Charles Dickens was bringing the horrors of such crimes to his readers in order to show how violent the times were – for poor people in particular. He was a social reformer. He wasn't a writer who merely wanted to line his own pockets; he wanted to improve society. Can you say the same, Mr Fothergill? You claim you are bringing great works of literature to the public, but that's not really the case. All you're doing is selling jigsaws and making a fortune out of murder.'

'Hardly a fortune, my dear, and –'

'Don't you call me "my dear". How dare you patronise me!'

Mr Fothergill had reddened in the face of this onslaught.

'I can assure you I wasn't patronising you; I apologise if I gave that impression. But, really, when you say I'm making a fortune out of murder, aren't you exaggerating slightly? All kinds of entertainment have murder in them – films especially.'

'Yes, films especially,' agreed Ms King, who wasn't a bit appeased by Mr Fothergill's apology. 'Children are constantly assaulted with film after film containing violent action. Is it any wonder we're seeing an increase in violence in schools – ?'

So far, Don Clement hadn't needed to intervene to keep the conversation flowing, but he did now.

'What's your evidence for that? You say violence is increasing in schools, but is that true?'

Mr Fothergill was hardly aware of Ms King's reply; he was trying to come to terms with everything she had said in attacking him. How aggressive she was! How bitter! He found himself wondering if she had a good sex life – but only fleetingly because now he was being addressed again.

'He looks smart, doesn't he?' Melissa observed to her mother. 'I wonder if he's got his bowler hat with him. I bet he has. He always brings it to work. I don't remember seeing him in that suit before, though. Saving it up for special occasions like this, I suppose.'

Joan had just switched on her television. She'd been washing her hair and had forgotten all about the programme till it was already underway. She hadn't even dried her hair yet. It was still damp and bedraggled, and in that state did nothing for her looks. If she hadn't been pretty before, she was even less pretty now. And because she was using a hair drier she had to keep switching it off so she could hear Mr Fothergill whenever he was speaking. She wasn't bothered what the woman was saying. She wasn't really bothered what Mr Fothergill was saying, but she did believe in loyalty, so she listened to him.

Mr Millar with an 'a' wished his wife would stop asking him questions while he was trying to listen to what both Mr Fothergill and the woman were saying. He kept raising his hand to silence her till he'd heard what particularly interested him. It worked for a while, but Mrs Millar was obviously someone who believed that it was only by asking questions that one got to know anything.

Don Clement was asking Mr Fothergill whether he intended to carry on with his murder series.

'With our *Two Puzzles and One Murder* series? Of course. We know from correspondence that many people are enjoying trying to work out which murders are being depicted. Why, I even have one letter here' – he produced an envelope from his inside pocket and extracted the letter from it – 'which is a good example of the interest that has been generated in the literature from which the murders are taken.' He waved the letter in the air.

'Can you read it to us?' asked Clement.

'No, that wouldn't be right. I don't have the person's permission. But it's from a gentleman who lives in the north of England and who has written to me a few times desperate to know which works of literature we are using. He obviously isn't a well-read man, so I'm only happy that he is starting to take an interest in literature because of our jigsaws.'

'Did you tell him which works of literature you had used?'

'No, absolutely not. That was our policy from the start. We wanted to get people talking about –'

'Of course you did,' Ms King broke in again. 'You wanted more and more people to hear about your jigsaws and buy them. And it's the people who are interested in murder who will. You're feeding their habit. You're as bad as those drug dealers who constantly supply junkies with their –'

'That's a bit over the top, isn't it?' suggested Clement.

'No, it isn't. It may be a more subtle form of addiction, but violence insinuates itself into one's psyche in all kinds of ways; we hardly notice it's there till we become violent ourselves. I have a bad temper – and that's a form of violence I try to control but occasionally fail to do so. And if even I, an adult who despairs of violence, can be violent, think how violent our children can become when violence is seen as a way of achieving self-esteem, as it very often is with boys in particular.'

Mr Fothergill suddenly remembered something else he had intended to mention.

'Are we still talking about jigsaws?' This he said with a baffled expression. 'Or are we talking about things like water pistols, which, I think you'll agree are much more dangerous than any jigsaw.'

'Water pistols *are* dangerous – physically. Jigsaws are dangerous mentally. And the damage we do mentally to our children is, I suggest, more dangerous than what any jet of water might do.'

'Even if it knocks a child's eye out?'

Ms King didn't reply. For a moment, she was taken aback by Mr Fothergill's comment. He realised this and sought to take advantage.

'Our jigsaws are harmless and educational and good fun. We are testing those people who have a good knowledge of literature and those who would like to know more. At the same time, we wanted to initiate discussions about the works of literature we were using. But we haven't made it easy for them. Why, in our last jigsaw we even – maybe I shouldn't be telling you this – we even included a red herring. I won't say what it was; that would spoil the fun for those people who haven't worked it out yet –'

Ms King saw a chance to retrieve her position.

'It was the book by Tolstoy,' she declared. 'You put a book by Tolstoy in the picture, even though the murder came from a novel by Dostoevsky – *Crime and Punishment*. That was the red herring.'

Mr Fothergill was flabbergasted.

'Really, Ms King, I think that was most unfair.'

'The first jigsaw was a scene from *Oliver Twist*; the second was Othello's murder of Desdemona in Shakespeare's *Othello* –'

'Mr Clement, I must protest. If I'd known Ms King was going to do this – to reveal to your viewers what the murders in my jigsaws are, I would never have agreed to –'

'The third one was the murder in *The Murder of Roger Ackroyd* by Agatha Christie.' Ms King sat back with satisfaction.

'That was uncalled for, Ms King,' said Clement belatedly.

'No, it wasn't. It was very much called for. Perhaps now the public won't see the need to buy any more of these wretched and violent jigsaws.'

Melissa's mouth had dropped open. Her mother, who had false teeth, kept hers shut. George started shaking his head. Chester gave Ms King a 'V' sign. Joan had switched on her drier again when Ms King had interrupted Mr Fothergill, so she hadn't heard everything she said. Mr Millar with an 'a' said nothing; and even his wife merely looked at him, wondering if what that woman had done would be a threat to his job.

That was unlikely. But after what had been revealed in the programme, another threat was more likely. A threat of a more violent kind.

Edgar Rice Root was staring at his television screen. His eyes were round and hate-filled. He was still digesting what that chap Fothergill had said.

A red herring.

A red herring in the fourth jigsaw.

And according to that woman it was the book by Tolstoy.

The murder in the jigsaw had not occurred in a novel by Tolstoy: it had occurred in one by that other guy, whatever his name was. *Crime and Punishment* – that was the title of the novel.

Crime and Punishment.

Not *War and Peace*. Not *Anna Karenina*. Not *Resurrection*.

All that reading had been a waste of time.

And all because that chap had been making a fool of him.

A fool of him, Edgar Rice Root.

He shouldn't have done that. Not with a red herring.

And wasn't that one of *his* letters the chap had been waving about?

Edgar felt murderous.

He was still watching the television screen as the programme came to an end but he'd long ceased to hear anything – except the words 'a red herring', which echoed screechingly in his mind.

Tolstoy was a red herring.

There was no murder in any of his novels which matched the murder in the jigsaw. The one he'd been looking for was in that other guy's … *Crime and Punishment*.

Edgar had to keep repeating the fact to truly believe it.

And all thanks to that chap.

Fothergill. Andrew Fothergill.

His next murder victim.

Chapter 20

An Unexpected Supposition

Fullerton had eventually given a helping hand to Carter with the jigsaw. He'd had to. Carter was having so much trouble with *No. 2* that when the inspector noticed an obvious fit he impatiently pointed it out and then was hooked. He spotted another one and then another. It wasn't all plain sailing, though. He too had great difficulty with the bed cover, more than once taking a piece off Carter because he thought he knew where it should go, only to find he was wrong, whereupon Carter would take the piece back – with a certain annoyance – because he thought he knew, only to find that he didn't either.

They were both annoyed when Constable Feeney popped in and suggested that a particular piece went 'there', only to find that he was as wrong as they had been.

'You're wasting our time, Feeney,' barked Fullerton. 'Disappear!'

In revenge, Feeney spread it about at the station that Fullerton and Carter were doing jigsaws instead of solving crimes. It must have seemed that way, for neither Fullerton nor Carter had explained to anyone exactly what they were doing. Nor was it entirely clear that Carter for one actually knew.

But eventually all the pieces were put together. The picture was there to see. A murder scene. They didn't know where it came from. Carter's wife, being no lover of Shakespeare, hadn't worked it out yet. What interested Fullerton, however, was the scene itself and in particular what clues it contained. There had been a seeming coincidence between the clues in jigsaw *No. 1* and those planted at one of the murders he was investigating, and between those in jigsaw *No. 3* and those planted at another of the murders he was investigating, so … it might be, he reasoned, that there would be another seeming coincidence between the clues in *No. 2* and those at a third murder.

And sure enough – the pillow over the face of the victim.

'Didn't you notice that when you first did the jigsaw,' Fullerton scolded Carter.

'What, sir?'

'The pillow.'

'What about it?'

'It's on the face of the victim. She's obviously been suffocated. Doesn't it remind you of anything?'

Carter looked down at pillow.

'Actually, yes, sir. That woman who was murdered –'

'Yes, Carter – that woman. And the other jigsaws. Remember the clues in those? The dog with the red legs, the ring –'

'Yes, sir. I said it was a strange coincidence. And this seems to confirm it.'

'Confirm what?'

'What a coincidence it is. To have three jigsaws –'

'Carter, you're a blithering idiot. Can you not see the difference between a coincidence and a clue? It is not a coincidence that the clues in the jigsaws match clues that have been planted at various murder scenes: it's a deliberate act of humour on the part of the murderer. Can't you see that?'

'If you're sure they've been planted there deliberately, yes, I can see that. But I don't –'

'Don't, Carter!' snapped Fullerton, raising his hand. 'Say no more. Keep your thoughts to yourself. We're making progress at last. I'm not sure what all this means yet, but … let's get started on jigsaw *No. 4*.'

Mrs Fothergill was full of praise for her husband's performance during the debate. She couldn't wait to get home and watch it again. They seldom recorded programmes but this one they had. Mr Fothergill was eager to see it too. He remained modest in the face of his wife's compliments, but he wouldn't have had to be tortured to admit to being pleased with the defence he'd made against what at times had seemed disproportionate attacks, to say the least.

'I don't wish to sound rude,' he told his wife as they drove home, 'but she was a bit of a tartar, that woman. I didn't hear a friendly word from her either before the discussion or after it.'

'She's a fanatic,' Mrs Fothergill replied. 'She's got a bee in her bonnet about those jigsaws and won't listen to anybody who argues against her. I think you put her in her place all right.'

That remark pleased Mr Fothergill. Putting Ms Stella King in her place was exactly what he'd been hoping to do.

And their viewing of the recording – with Mr Fothergill squirming in embarrassment at the sight of himself on television – appeared to confirm that he had been the victor; which was also the view of members of Fothergill's staff who said as much the following morning. Melissa didn't exactly confirm it but told Mr Fothergill she thought he'd looked very smart. Chester said he'd made that woman look silly. George complimented him for handling himself very well during what must have been a daunting experience. Even Alysse managed a few words, expressing her favourable reaction. And Joan, on greeting Mr Fothergill at reception, enthused immoderately, bearing in mind that she'd been more interested in drying her hair than in anything he had said.

It was all good to hear ... and yet, wondered Mr Fothergill once he was alone in his office, wasn't it all too good to be true? He could expect support and approval from his wife and the people who worked for him, who after all were involved in the production of the jigsaws, but what about the general public? Had they been as impressed with his side of the argument, or had they been more convinced by Ms King's? And would they continue to buy the jigsaws now that the wretched woman had revealed what the murders were?

That was the key question for which he, as a businessman, needed an answer. Time would tell, he supposed. For the moment, all he could do was wait and see … and think of a murder for a fifth jigsaw. It was time to give some thought to that.

Fullerton and Carter were still working on *Two Puzzles and One Murder No.4*. They took some satisfaction in finishing it rather more quickly than they had *No. 2*, but once it was done they were just as much at a loss to identify the murder as they had been with *No. 2*. Naturally, however, they spotted an obvious clue. Or, rather, Fullerton did. He jabbed a finger at the book by Tolstoy on the table.

'There, Carter – that makes it obvious, I think. The murder was committed in a novel by Tolstoy. That means it could be *War and Peace* or that other one he's famous for … *Anna Karenina*, is it?

Something like that. Have you read them? Or should I ask whether you walked to the moon last week?'

'No, sir; I haven't. I always meant to read *War and Peace*, but –'

'But you haven't got round to it. Anyway, it doesn't matter. See that, Carter?' He pointed out another object in the picture. 'Do you know what that is?"

'Some kind of sign, sir.'

'Obviously. But do you know what kind of sign?'

'No, sir.'

'It's a pawnbroker's sign. Clearly the murder takes place at a pawnbroker's..... Which tells us what?'

Carter looked blank.

'It tells us that the person murdered was probablya pawnbroker. And from that we can conclude what?' Fullerton now stared at Carter in a most challenging sort of way.

Carter looked blank but miserable.

'It tells us that the next murder on our patch will very likely be of a pawnbroker.'

'Why do you think that, sir?'

'Because there are matches in the first three jigsaws with three of the murders we've been investigating. Some twisted mind has decided to repeat the murders in the jigsaws by murdering people in real life in the same way. Can't you see that? Why else would the clues in the jigsaws match the clues we found at the murder scenes?'

The penny dropped.

'I see what you mean, sir. Yes, you're right. They do match. I should have realised that myself when I did the first jigsaw with Ryan. I did notice the dog with red legs –'

'But you didn't see the link between that dog and the one at the house of that murdered woman. Not to worry, Carter. You've learnt how to do jigsaws pretty well. Next we'll try to get you up to scratch as a detective. Now … what's the first thing we have to do now?'

Carter felt like saying they should put the jigsaws back in their boxes so he could take them back to his little boy, but he thought better of it. He pulled a face indicating that he wasn't sure.

'Do you know any pawnbrokers, Carter?'

'I believe there is one not too far from where I live. I've never been there myself but –'

'But you will be going there before the day's out. The fact is, Carter, that whoever the pawnbroker is, his life may be in danger, and you are going to warn him.'

'Warn him?'

'That someone might be coming to chop him up with an axe. Look – what's that there?' Fullerton jabbed the jigsaw violently, causing one or two pieces to become loose.

'An axe, sir.'

'Yes, an axe. The murder weapon – obviously. We can't sit about doing nothing while a killer is going about with an axe, looking for pawnbrokers. We'll have to warn all of them – all the pawnbrokers in our area. They're going to have to take precautions, whether they like it or not, even if they do hate the police. Most of them do, you know. I've had experience of pawnbrokers before. So … we need a list. You'd better look in *Yellow Pages* first – there'll be a few there.'

*

Within a few days numerous pawnbrokers around the North West had been advised to make doubly sure that their premises were locked at night and to keep an eye open for any suspicious-looking characters who might be about to attack them. Naturally, such a warning aroused some concern, and quite a few innocent people were scrutinised closely as they strolled past one shop or another. Horace Wopple, a fifty-year-old dealer in Preston, took the extreme measure of removing from his window a samurai sword, which was close to its expiry date for redeeming, and keeping it handy, not forgetting to take it up to his bedroom at night. More than once, hearing an unfamiliar noise, he seized hold of the sword for what he would have claimed at his trial afterwards were purposes of self-defence. Fortunately it didn't come to that, perhaps to his disappointment.

Other pawnbrokers felt the urge to get out of bed after midnight to check that they had locked their back doors – not a pleasant thing to have to do in the middle of winter, especially when they found, as they usually did, that the doors were not only locked but bolted as well.

Fullerton would have been amused to hear that and also pleased that they were acting on his advice. He hated being ignored. He liked to set things in motion and see them carried out. Most particularly, he liked to investigate and solve crimes. So far, he hadn't solved the 'jigsaw murders', as he now thought of them, but maybe, he thought, it might be worth while contacting the manufacturers of the jigsaws to ask them a few questions. For all he knew, the murderer might be someone who worked for the company or who was in some way involved with it. Unlikely perhaps, considering the company was based in London, but he had to follow up every possible line of inquiry.

Chapter 21

The Aftermath

Melissa loved Twitter. She liked to tweet and liked to read tweets made by other people. And since the television debate she had read them avidly, just to see what the response to it was. Daphne loved Twitter. She liked to tweet and liked to read tweets made by other people. And since the television debate she had read them just as much as Melissa. So it wasn't surprising that the two should be planning to share a flat; they did have common interests. But the difference in their reactions to the tweets they read indicated a future disharmony between them.

Daphne was mildly amused by how seriously those who condemned violence in all its forms were taking the jigsaws. Melissa was shocked by their comments, and one in particular sent her racing to Mr Fothergill. She had quite a job explaining to him what Twitter was, but when he finally grasped it, she repeated the extraordinary remark.

'"Jigsaws are the new terrorism."' Then she waited for his reaction.

'"Jigsaws are the new terrorism"?'

Melissa nodded. 'I'm sure he was joking, but it just goes to show, doesn't it?'

Mr Fothergill didn't know whether he was joking or not, and he wasn't sure what Miss Morgan meant when she said it just goes to show; but he didn't like it. 'Jigsaws are the new terrorism' – what nonsense! Of course it was joke; it couldn't be anything else. Unless the people on Twitter, whatever it was, were twits. Mr Fothergill took little satisfaction from this witticism; it was too serious a matter.

'What else have people been saying – or twittering or … whatever?'

'Tweeting – that's what call it. Oh, all kinds of things. Some of them have been tweeting in support of you.'

They're not all twits, then, thought Mr Fothergill.

Melissa chuckled. 'One of them said that woman should be hit over the head with one of the jigsaws; then she'd know what violence really was.'

Not an answer, thought Mr Fothergill. And he wasn't sure how it would work – hitting someone over the head with a jigsaw. All that would happen is that the pieces would break apart …

'There are hundreds of people tweeting, though,' said Melissa. 'I can't remember what they've all said.'

'Hundreds?' gasped Mr Fothergill. *That many twits, eh?* 'It must be popular, this Twitter.'

'Oh, it is. You should try it. You can give your opinions about anything you like –'

'I don't think so, Miss Morgan.' *Wouldn't want to be a twit like the rest of 'em.* 'I have quite enough to keep me busy, thank you – like putting a new jigsaw on the market; it's time we did that. We've been a bit lax in that respect for one reason or another. And there's no time like the present. So …call in Mr Miller with an 'e', Mr Millar with an 'a' …'

Thirty minutes later, the usual members of staff were gathered together in Mr Fothergill's office.

There was a buzz of excitement as they waited for Mr Fothergill to start the proceedings. They were just as keen as he was to get another jigsaw in the shops, if only to spite the likes of that woman. Melissa started telling everyone about the comments on Twitter. Daphne joined in, telling them of the comments she had read. And for a while there was competition between the two as to who could remember the silliest ones. But Melissa won that hands down with 'Jigsaws are the new terrorism'. Daphne hadn't seen that one, and although she laughed as much as anyone, she felt aggrieved at the fact that nothing she recalled provoked as much mirth. She felt bitter towards Melissa for that, and had Mr Fothergill not started speaking, her resentment might there and then have developed into hatred.

'I must confess,' Mr Fothergill began, 'I have tried to come up with a fifth murder, but I guess I'm not as well-read on murder stories as I thought. I didn't want us to repeat anything we'd done in the first four jigsaws, which meant disqualifying anything by Agatha Christie or Charles Dickens –'

'Or Shakespeare,' put in Chester.

'Or Shakespeare ... or, who was that other writer? ... that Russian chap ... Dostoevsky.'

'We could do a Tolstoy and Dostoevsky in reverse,' Chester suggested, bringing a puzzled look to everyone's face, excepting Mr Millar's. Chester explained. 'We could use a murder from one of Tolstoy's novels – I assume there is one – but put a novel by Dostoevsky in the picture ... as a red herring.'

There were grins all round.

'Ingenious, Mr Grounds,' allowed Mr Fothergill; 'but I don't think so. I can't believe there are many people who have read all those novels by Tolstoy and who would be doing our jigsaws. I think that's where we made a slight mistake before. Dostoevsky would have been a completely unknown writer for most in the jigsawing fraternity. Not that it wasn't a good idea,' he added, glancing at Alysse, 'but it must have proved particularly difficult for most people. Still ... a bit of difficulty never hurt anyone. The question now is: what next?'

George had been quiet so far, but now he raised a hand.

'I think I have the answer.'

'No more Shakespeare,' Chester reminded him.

'No more Shakespeare. In fact, one can't imagine anything more different from Shakespeare.' He paused, looking round at everyone. '*Little Red Riding Hood.*'

Chester burst into laughter. '*Little Red Riding Hood*!' It was an automatic response, which he now tried to justify. 'That's hardly from a great work of literature.'

George ignored him. 'Didn't you mention Grimms' fairy tales in your debate with that woman? And didn't she say she'd like to ban those – or stop children from reading them? It got me thinking. Why not do a fairy tale – or a folk tale, if that's what it is – as our next jigsaw. If she tried to ban that, she'd make herself look extremely stupid, bearing in mind the fairy tales themselves are available for children.'

Mr Fothergill became more and more elated as George went on.

'Yes! What a marvellous idea! You've done it again, Mr Miller. *Little Red Riding Hood*…. Oh, but what's the murder in that?'

'The wolf. It gets murdered – killed – by a woodsman, I believe.'

'Is that murder?' protested Chester.

'Same thing,' insisted George. 'And the wolf eats the granny, doesn't it? That's murder in a way.'

'What – eating a granny? Animals don't commit murder. They just eat people and other animals. You can't say that's murder. When we eat chicken legs, no one says we murdered the chickens first. We say we killed them ... or slaughtered them. Murder is something entirely different.'

Mr Fothergill was frowning. 'He does have a point, Mr Miller.'

'Not at all,' insisted George, slightly miffed that Mr Fothergill seemed to have changed sides. 'Whether it's actually murder or not is a fine distinction we don't have to make. It's killing most foul, whatever it is.'

'"Murder most foul" – isn't that the saying? And isn't it from Shakespeare? I bet it is. You've got Shakespeare on the brain, George. – Oh, I get it ... 'killing most foul' – you were talking about chickens and then you said 'killing most foul'. Hilarious, George – absolutely hilarious.'

George ignored Chester's sarcasm. 'We were discussing *Little Red Riding Hood* – and the wolf gets murdered – killed – slaughtered – chopped up, whatever you want to call it – at the end of the story. I don't see why we can't use it – if only to show that woman up.'

Chester immediately changed his tune. 'Well, I'm all for that. So yes, let's use it. *Little Red Riding Hood* it is.' He felt he had been more than a match for George in this little quarrel – as everyone, he thought, would agree – so he saw no reason not to be magnanimous in victory.

No one else made any objection or suggestion, so *Little Red Riding Hood* it was.

Mr Fothergill rubbed his hands together, eager to get production underway. But that was some way off. First, Mr Dawes would have to be advised of their decision, and he would have to paint the picture.

'Thank you, Mr Miller,' he said as the others made to leave. 'You're becoming quite an expert at making suggestions. If you think of any other murders we can use, please let me know.'

Alone again, Mr Fothergill wasted no time in phoning Mr Dawes. Whenever he did that, he was worried that no one would answer. That had happened on numerous occasions, and sometimes he'd had to make the call four or five times before catching Mr Dawes in – or, more probably, catching him in the right mood for a conversation, which wasn't always the case. Mercifully Gregory picked up the receiver this time. Had he been less inebriated he might not have done. His grunt was the drunken equivalent of 'Hello'.

'Mr Dawes, it's Andrew Fothergill.'

Grunt.

'How are you?'

Grunt.

'Enjoy your Christmas?'

Grunt.

'Good, good. I don't know whether you saw my television appearance when I discussed our jigsaws with that woman …'

Not even a grunt.

'She was complaining about our use of murders in our jigsaws, Can you imagine?'

No grunt, but a closing of the eyes as if Mr Dawes was about to fall asleep.

'Anyway, we've come up with an idea – or I should say that Mr Miller has – that's Mr Miller with an 'e', our financial expert. He suggested *Little Red Riding Hood*…' A pause for Gregory's reaction.

There was none.

'There was a dispute about whether the killing of the wolf was in fact a murder, but we decided it didn't really matter, not if it puts Ms King, that woman, in her place. After all, she'd look pretty foolish if she complained about a jigsaw depicting the wolf's slaying – yes, slaying, that's what it is, I suppose – when in fact the tale of *Little Red Riding Hood* is already available to children in books.'

Gregory grunted as he slowly came to realise he was talking to someone on the phone.

So … we'd like you to paint a picture in your usual way, with clues and so on, of the murder – or the slaying, whatever we should call it. If you've forgotten the story, I'm sure you'll be able to check it in the local library; they're bound to have it in the children's section. Can you manage that?'

A grunt confirming he could.

'That's fine. I would appreciate the finished picture as soon as possible. Is a week from now all right?'

A grunt, either confirming that it was or insisting that he'd need much longer to do a good one.

Whichever it was, Mr Fothergill seemed delighted.

'Excellent. Let me know as soon as you've completed it and I'll arrange the usual get-together. Good day to you.'

Not even a grunt.

For precisely ten minutes Mr Fothergill felt inordinately pleased with life. He went and stood by the window, gazing outside with a broad smile on his face. It was all a fuss about nothing, he thought. By the time *Two Puzzles and One Murder No. 5* appeared in the shops, he'd have forgotten all about Ms Stella King, and she – probably – would have forgotten all about his jigsaws. She'd have other axes to grind – with filmmakers, for instance. She'd vilified them during the debate. And, truth to tell, she had legitimate concerns over some of the films being made these days – explicit films showing gruesome and bloody violence. He didn't watch such films himself but he would have been a fool not to know they existed. How could his jigsaws be compared to that sort of stuff?

Then his ten minutes were up, and Melissa spoke over the intercom.

'Mr Fothergill, there's a phone call for you.' She sounded worried. 'From a Detective Inspector Fullerton.'

Mr Fothergill had returned to his desk. 'A detective inspector?' He sounded the same. 'What does he want?'

'I've no idea. He didn't say.'

'Oh, well you better put him through, then.' All kinds of thing were racing through Mr Fothergill's head. Had he done something wrong – like producing violent jigsaws and putting them in shops, where they could be bought by children, who were then influenced by them to be violent themselves? It wasn't a serious consideration but it was there in his mind.

'Mr Fothergill?' Inspector Fullerton's voice came over loud and clear.

'Yes.' Mr Fothergill's was rather shaky.

'I'm Inspector Fullerton …' Mr Fothergill didn't grasp the inspector's opening words; he was still wondering what on earth he could want. 'Your company has been manufacturing a series of jigsaws entitled *Two Puzzles and One Murder*. Is that right?'

'Yes.'

Fullerton went on to describe – unnecessarily, since he was speaking to the man who made them – what the pictures in the jigsaws represented.

'Yes,' Mr Fothergill repeated.

'Murders taken from works of fiction – is that right?'

'Yes.'

'What would you say, Mr Fothergill, if I told you that those murders are being turned into real-life murders?'

Mr Fothergill didn't say anything for a moment. He could hardly believe what he'd been asked, so he wasn't ready yet to offer a reply.

Mr Fullerton didn't say anything for more than a moment. He was used to waiting longer than someone else to talk first, and he was damned if he'd let a manufacturer of jigsaws prove more stubborn than he was. Mr Fothergill didn't.

'Turned into real-life murders?'

'Yes.'

'What on earth do you mean?'

Fullerton grimaced in exasperation. 'Well, put simply, someone is murdering people and leaving clues matching those in your jigsaws.'

Mr Fothergill was staggered – and speechless.

'He's obviously a murderer with a sick sense of humour,' Fullerton continued; 'but that doesn't mean we can let him have his fun. It's my job to stop him, capture him and put him behind bars.'

'Of course,' Mr Fothergill finally managed to say.

'To be honest, Mr Fothergill, when I decided to phone you, I thought you might be able to help in that respect; but I doubt you can. All the murders are up here in the North West. There's no reason to think you know anything that could assist me in my inquiries. However … there is one thing you can do.'

'Oh?'

'Are you planning any more jigsaws in this series?'

'Indeed, yes. I've just arranged to have a fifth jigsaw prepared.'

'Hmmm. It would be better if you postponed it … till after the murderer has been caught. We wouldn't want him copying that one as well.'

'But that's impossible, Inspector. We have a business to run. Our jigsaws are very popular. To delay production now would be detrimental to our sales.'

'Frankly, Mr Fothergill, as Clark Gable said in *Gone with the Wind*, I don't give a damn. I don't want you to do anything that would tempt him to commit another murder.'

'Inspector, I can put your mind at rest in that respect. Our next jigsaw is actually from a folk tale concerning a wolf. I doubt your murderer would think of murdering a wolf.'

Fullerton wondered he was talking to an imbecile.

'What exactly is the murder you're talking about?'

'Ah, I'm afraid I can't be more explicit. We have a policy not to reveal which murders we're depicting in the jigsaws.'

Fullerton decided he *was* talking to an imbecile.

'Mr Fothergill, I don't particularly care which murder it is. All I care about is that you postpone production of it till' – his voice was rising – 'we get the murderer.'

Mr Fothergill heard the more strident tone coming from the other end of the line.

'Yes, but it could take years before you catch him. The police aren't always quick to make arrests –'

'No, indeed. And that's often because the public aren't very helpful. They impede us in our investigations. I'm sure you wouldn't want to do that.'

'I wouldn't. But for the life of me, I can't see how not postponing production of our latest jigsaw would impede your investigation.'

'It would, Mr Fothergill, because after it's been on sale for a couple of weeks, we would probably have another murder to investigate, which would mean more work for everyone here. Comprenez?' Fullerton realised he'd used a foreign word. He hated himself for doing it. He hated Carter for infecting him with the habit. He hated the French for having such a word … if it was French.

Mr Fothergill understood the word. And it did worry him that someone might commit another murder simply because –

Suddenly a flash of misguided inspiration seized him.

'Wait a minute! This is a hoax, isn't it? You're working with that woman. You're so determined to stop production of our jigsaws that you're pretending to be a detective –'

'Mr Fothergill – I assure you I am a detective. Detective Inspector Fullerton. You can check my credentials by phoning back, if you insist.'

Mr Fothergill was glaring at the phone in his hand.

'I don't think so, Mr whoever you are. There's not a policeman on the planet who would expect me to stop production of a jigsaw on that pretext. And there's not a murderer on the planet who would do what you've suggested one of them has done. But I compliment you, sir, on your vivid imagination. You should write crime novels.' Having said which, he slammed the phone down.

Having done which, he returned to the window, folded his arms and gazed outside with a very uncharacteristic scowl on his face.

Chapter 22

Production Thwarted

Fullerton stared at the phone in his hand. The man had hung up. He couldn't believe it. Here he was, conducting an investigation into the murders of a number of elderly people, and this … this Fothergill had accused him of being a hoaxer. Fullerton forced himself to laugh incredulously. Then he stopped. He'd meant to ask him for a rundown of the sales of his jigsaws in all the shops around the country. Whoever the murderer was, he must have bought the jigsaws from somewhere, and he must have bought all of them. If a sales assistant could remember a suspicious- or weird-looking customer … Well, it was possible. It would have been useful to have a list of where the jigsaws had been sold.

Fullerton wondered whether to phone the man again. He was reluctant to do so. He didn't like having to chase after people like that, but ... he was an investigator. With a growl, he made the call again.

Only to find that Mr Fothergill refused to accept it.

'I don't take calls from hoaxers,' he told Melissa.

'But what if he wasn't a hoaxer?' Mrs Fothergill asked him later. 'There have been a lot of murders in Lancashire in the last few years. We've spoken about them, haven't we?'

'Yes, but isn't it a bit fanciful that there should be clues at the murder scenes which matched those in our jigsaws? What murderer, for heaven's sake, is going to spend his time doing jigsaws?' Mr Fothergill started chuckling. 'Why, it's preposterous, Vera. And the idea that a murderer will stop murdering people because we've stopped producing jigsaws is ... well, it's farcical.'

'You could have phoned the police station where the caller said he's based and checked whether he was genuine or not.'

Mr Fothergill hesitated to admit that this was what his caller had suggested.

'The fact is, Vera, I'm not sure I wanted to know he was genuine. I really don't see how it matters one jot to a murderer whether we give him a jigsaw to copy or not. He could just as easily copy some other jigsaw –'

'Not with clues in them, like ours.'

'No, well, even so …' Mr Fothergill was floundering. He didn't appreciate the fact that his wife was making him feel uncomfortable. Murder was a serious matter, and if –

It didn't bear thinking about. He should have listened to the man. If the chap was a detective, and if –

He couldn't bring himself to think it.

Even his own wife seemed to be suggesting that if someone else was murdered, he, Andrew Fothergill, her husband, would be partly responsible. Might be best, he decided, if he did check. He could phone – where was it? –Preston, and ask if they knew a Detective Inspector Fullerton, and if they did …

'I'll phone tomorrow,' he said. 'No harm in checking. You're quite right.'

*

That same evening, at his kitchen table, Edgar Rice Root was cutting up a large piece of cardboard – found in his garage – into a 24-inch square. Having done that, he picked up a compass with a pencil in it and drew three circles on the cardboard. They were each six inches in diameter, and in the form of an inverted triangle, with two circles lying horizontally above the other. So far so good, but now he had to decide which colour to use to fill them in, and he wasn't sure what colour they usually were. Something told him they should be gold; but since the cardboard was a light brown, gold wouldn't provide much contrast and the balls wouldn't show up well. He wasn't the type to bother too much about the right and wrong of things, so he picked up a black marker and used that. Finally, he linked the three balls together with a frame joined to a perpendicular representing a wall.

It was a pawnbroker's sign.

The following morning, when Mr Fothergill asked Melissa to contact the police at Preston so he could speak to the inspector who had phoned him, her mouth dropped open, confirming that something had shocked her to the core. She didn't tell Mr Fothergill what it was, but it was partly his fault – even wholly his fault. He had told her that he didn't take calls from hoaxers – that was what he'd said. So naturally she had assumed that the man claiming to be an inspector was not one, and equally naturally she had later informed Daphne that Mr Fothergill was starting to receive phone calls from hoaxers who, they decided, were probably supporters of that woman and were out to sabotage jigsaw production at Fothergill's. If the man really was an inspector …

Melissa discovered that he was, and, after putting the call through to Mr Fothergill, would have hurried to the office where Daphne was working and let her know that she'd been mistaken. The trouble was that it was Daphne's day off again, so as things turned out she didn't find out for a few days, and then not from Melissa but from Chester. All of which went down very badly with Daphne and caused a row between her and Melissa which ended any possibility that they would share a flat.

When Melissa put Inspector Fullerton through to Mr Fothergill, the latter couldn't apologise enough.

'That's all right, Mr Fothergill. We all make fools of ourselves at times. The important thing is that we work together to bring the murderer to justice.'

'Indeed, Inspector. But I'm still not convinced that ceasing production of our jigsaws – even temporarily – would stop his killing spree. If he has it in him to –'

'Believe me, Mr Fothergill, it would. But even if there's nothing certain about that, it might. It might. And surely that's a good enough reason for us to try it. Why don't we agree not to put on sale any more of those particular jigsaws for, what, six months? That would give us –'

'Six months!' exclaimed Mr Fothergill. 'But that could damage our company irreparably. These jigsaws have been very popular. We couldn't hope to replace their sales with anything else, not in the immediate future. It could mean job losses … a shorter working week …'

'Oh, come, Mr Fothergill, I'm sure you're exaggerating. The jigsaws you already have in the shops will continue to sell if they're as popular as you say. We're talking murder here, Mr Fothergill.' Fullerton's had become firmer. 'I'm trying to be sympathetic, but apprehending a murderer is far more important – I think you'll agree – than selling jigsaws.'

Mr Fothergill didn't like that. Of course he agreed, but he failed to see why the police couldn't apprehend the murderer while his company was selling a *new* jigsaw.

'Six months seems far too long, Inspector. I'm sure you're capable of bringing the murderer to justice before then.' There was a bitterness in his tone now, but if Fullerton detected it he ignored it.

'Six months may seem too long to those outside the force, Mr Fothergill. But only to them. Those of us who have to bring criminals to trial know how difficult our job is. If other people can't appreciate that, then too bad; but it merely shows a lack of understanding on their part.'

This was definitely a dig at Mr Fothergill, who couldn't help but be aware of it. He had to give in, and he did. Six months it was.

He also agreed to let Fullerton have a rundown on the sales of the jigsaws in shops in Lancashire. To have done the same for shops all over the country would have been pointless; there were too many to check. Providing the list was a job for George, so once his conversation with Fullerton ended, Mr Fothergill asked for Mr

Miller with an 'e' to come to his office. While he was waiting for him to arrive, he also thought of Mr Dawes. Just the day before, he had asked him to paint a picture for *Two Puzzles and One Murder No.5* and to do it as soon as he could. That hardly seemed necessary now. And it wouldn't be right to have him give all his time to a painting for a jigsaw that couldn't be marketed for six months; he did paint other things as well. Best to phone him and say the painting wasn't as urgent as he'd previously said.

So he phoned him straight away.

'Hello, Mr Dawes,' he began. 'About the painting for the *Little Red Riding Hood* jigsaw …'

Gregory didn't know what he was talking about.

That same afternoon, Edgar Rice Root called in at Smith's in Blackpool. He was looking for a particular book. He didn't find it in Smith's, so he walked down to Waterstone's, which was situated behind the Tower. Edgar hardly noticed that. He'd lived in Blackpool all his life, and only now and then did he register its existence. Even now, despite its soaring proximity, it might well have been invisible. He entered Waterstone's and started his search.

This time he was lucky. He found a copy of the book he wanted, and in hardback. In a new translation.

Not that Edgar Rice Root cared about that!

But he bought it anyway ... which meant he now had everything he needed.

He already had an axe.

Chapter 23

A New Project

When word spread through the building that production would have to be put back for as much as six months, spirits sank and despondency set in. Mr Fothergill had always nurtured and encouraged in his company an ethos of teamwork, and everyone involved in the making and selling of the jigsaws and other puzzles felt deprived of a part of their lives. Mr Fothergill hadn't been exaggerating when he told Fullerton of the risk of a shorter working week for some of his employees. The company had enjoyed a successful year, but financially in an age of austerity no business could afford to ignore falls in sales, even when – or especially when – they were self-inflicted. It hadn't yet reached the stage when Mr

Fothergill would seriously have to consider cutbacks, but much would depend on how well the company managed to persuade retailers to take stock of other things they supplied. Melissa was quick to suggest that they bring out her favourite jigsaw again, one that had been stopped two years before.

'The one with rabbits on,' she reminded Mr Fothergill. 'There were I don't know how many of them – all supposedly hopping about in a field. It looked so funny – all those heads and long ears. It made me laugh just to look at them.'

'Yes, I remember it. I liked it too. But it did suffer a drop in popularity. I think children got frustrated with trying to sort out one long ear from another. From what I was told, they didn't enjoy doing it as much as grown-ups did.'

It was Chester who came up with the idea that impressed Mr Fothergill enough for him to give the go-ahead for it: a 4-for-3 offer. Or, as Mr Fothergill himself modified it, a 3-for-2 offer. Chester said it would persuade retailers to send in more orders for the first four of the *Two Puzzles and One Murder* series, when they might have been looking for newer merchandise to sell. Mr Fothergill made the change to his suggestion because he thought the retailers could pass it on more easily to their customers, especially those who had previously bought only one of the series.

And just for good measure Chester also suggested that they do a series of jigsaws based on folk tales or fairy tales that didn't involve murder or killing of any sort.

'In fact,' he said with a cunning air not discerned by Mr Fothergill, 'it might be better if we forget altogether about including the *Little Red Riding Hood* jigsaw in the murder series. We could use it in this other series.'

Mr Fothergill couldn't understand why they hadn't thought of that before.

'An excellent idea, Mr Grounds. We could go right ahead with it. All we need to do is to give the series a different name … like, say, *Two Puzzles and One Folk Tale* … or *Fairy Tale*. I say that because, naturally, we wouldn't reveal to the public which folk tale or fairy tale is being depicted. Inspector Fullerton can't object to that, I'm sure. It would guarantee steady full-time work for our people. Yes, Mr Grounds, we'll do it. And we'll make *Little Red Riding Hood* our first one … *Two Puzzles and One Folk Tale No. 1.*'

Melissa was the first to hear about this new project, and she was delighted.

'I've still got a large book of fairy tales from when I was a little girl. I'll check in that to see what stories we can use.'

'By all means do,' Mr Fothergill encouraged her. 'The more tales we have from which to select, the more likely it is we'll choose really good ones. I'm very enthusiastic about this. The jigsaws will be aimed primarily at children, and that, I suppose, is how it should be. So it might be a good idea if on the box we have a child – or two children, one boy and one girl – looking through a magnifying glass at the possible clues. Rather like the box cover for the *Two Puzzles and One Murder* series, but different enough for people to know it's a different series.'

Unsurprisingly, one person who had misgivings about the new project was George. He took offence at the 'daylight robbery', as he stupidly thought of it, of his suggestion of *Little Red Riding Hood* to be used for a different series of jigsaws from the one he'd intended. He made his feelings known to Mr Fothergill.

'In any case,' he added, 'I think you'll find folk tales have been used for jigsaws before. Many many times. We're hardly being original. More like copycats, if you ask me.'

'Yes,' agreed Mr Fothergill. 'I'm sure they have been used before – but never in the way we're going to use them. The children who do the jigsaws will have to work out from the clues we give them which folk tales they are. That, if I may say so, is becoming our unique selling point.'

George, of course, was not mollified. And when he learnt who was responsible for this change of plan, he was *determined* not to be mollified.

The same could be said of Edgar Rice Root. He was determined not to be mollified in respect of Mr Fothergill's red herring. And whereas George did a bit of sulking, Edgar still felt murderous. Whereas George complained to his fellow spiritualists about how badly he felt he was being treated at Fothergill's, Edgar was planning in secret to commit another murder. And whereas George was seriously considering whether to resign from Fothergill's because of all the mockery and underhand treatment he had to endure, Edgar was arranging a week's holiday from his job so that he could go down to London to carry out the murderous plan he had in mind (though he didn't mention that to his boss as the reason for his request).

Meanwhile, Inspector Fullerton had detectives all around the county visiting the shops on the list that Fothergill's had provided. It was a job they were paid to do. It was part of an investigation into murders that had been committed in their area. They were investigating officers and they had every right to do it. All that made sense, so no one could blame Fullerton for sending them on what other people might regard as a wild goose chase. The idea that sales assistants would remember every Tom, Dick and murderer who bought a jigsaw was optimistic at best. And yet it could have happened. There may well have been a scowling, glowering, evil-eyed, fist-clenching, tight-lipped, gravelly-voiced killer-type who stayed in a particular assistant's mind for months and months until a rather weary detective called in at the shop where she worked and asked if she could remember any such person. But it didn't happen. And a lot of abuse was hurled in Fullerton's distant direction by many detectives during the week in which they carried out their futile inquiries.

George was sitting alone at a table in the canteen when Joan entered. At another table Melissa was talking to Chester, Mr Millar and one of the young men from Mr Millar's production team. To spite Melissa, knowing that she and Daphne had fallen out again, Joan bought a sandwich from the counter and then went to sit with George; she hadn't shared a table with Melissa for some time and wasn't going to start now.

'You look fed up, George,' she said as she slipped into the seat opposite his.

George glanced up, surprised and not exactly pleased that she'd joined him. But it would have been rude not to answer and even ruder to lie.

'I am, to be honest.'

'Oh? What's the trouble?'

George hesitated. He needed a bit more encouragement.

'What's the matter?' Joan persisted.

'Spite – that's what the matter is.' He cocked his head towards the table where Chester was sitting. Joan had no doubt that Chester was the person indicated. 'My idea for a *Little Red Riding Hood* jigsaw …'

Joan didn't know anything about that; she never attended production meetings, being 'only' – as she often thought of it when such meetings were called – a receptionist.

'Chester went behind my back and persuaded Mr Fothergill to use it for something else. Spite … sheer spite – that's all it was.'

Joan's expression became grim and disapproving. 'There's no need for that. No need for spite. I can't stand people who do things out of spite. It's nasty.' She looked towards Melissa, but immediately turned away when she saw that Melissa was looking towards her.

'That's the way he is,' said George, warming to her sympathy. 'He's got to be top dog. He can't stand it when someone has a better idea than anything he he's had, so he's got to put a spanner in the works. I wonder at times whether I want to work with someone like that … whether I should start looking for employment elsewhere.'

'What – leave Fothergill's?' Joan was genuinely shocked. George had been at the company for far longer than she had. 'You can't do that, George. Fothergill's wouldn't be the same without you.'

'Nice of you to say so,' said George, sincerely appreciating the remark. 'But there is a limit to what one can put up with – or *should* put up with for the sake of one's dignity.'

'Well, I've always thought of you as having dignity, George. You're the most dignified man here at Fothergill's, including Mr Fothergill himself, if you ask me.

'Thank you, Joan. It's very kind of you. It makes a change from all the snide comments I'm used to hearing.'

'Oh, I'm sure half of them are in fun. Chester can't help himself. He's got to have a witty remark for every situation.'

'I don't mind remarks made in fun; it's when they're snide or spiteful, that's when I object. Then they're not fun, they're vicious.'

'I couldn't agree more, if they are snide or spiteful. All I'm saying is, don't jump to hasty conclusions. People often fall out because one of them's jumped to the wrong conclusion. Always count to ten, George, before you come to any conclusion – that's my motto.' She chuckled. 'I never stop counting to ten, me. One two three four five six seven eight nine ten – that's me all day.'

George grunted. 'I could count to a hundred as far as Chester's concerned and I'd still come to the same conclusion – and the right one. He's spiteful.'

Just then someone else arrived at their table: Daphne.

'Mind if I join you?' she asked, pulling out a chair so she could sit in it.

Joan was delighted. It wasn't so much that Daphne was joining them as that she wasn't joining Melissa. They were obviously still at loggerheads.

'What a relief, eh?'

Something had put her in good spirits. Joan didn't particularly want to talk to her, but she raised her eyebrows inquisitively.

'I was really worried when we had to stop producing that murder series,' Daphne explained. 'I thought I might be laid off. I was taken on only because you were doing so well with it. Then when we had to stop it, I figured I might be the one who had to go.

Last to be employed, first to be sacked. Thank goodness Chester suggested this new series we're doing.'

George and Joan merely stared at Daphne, saying nothing. Daphne became conscious of their attitude. She thought perhaps she'd sounded selfish.

'Of course, I suppose nobody's job was safe,' she added quickly. 'Not even yours, George. How long have you been here?'

She waited for and expected an answer. George wondered whether he should give her one.

'Fifteen years,' he said at last.

'How long have you, Joan?' Daphne felt the need to bring them both into the conversation.

'Not as long as that,' said Joan, determined not to be brought into it too deeply.

'Yes, well, even you two …'

Her sentence faded away, to be replaced by an outburst from George which attracted the attention of everyone in the canteen.

'Maybe you think', he began, getting aggressively to his feet and pushing his chair back, 'we should go over there and thank him on our bended knees for the great favour he's done us.' His voice was shrill with the intense irritation he felt. Then he stomped out of the canteen.

Daphne's mouth dropped open, confirming that she'd never seen anything like that before. Joan's eyes opened wide, confirming that she too had never seen anything like it, but also that she wasn't about to copy someone like Daphne just because she was prettier than she was.

Melissa's mouth dropped open at the other table, confirming that she was about to come over to see what had happened to upset George so much, as indeed she did. She could see that Daphne was responsible, and wanted to know all about it.

'What on earth's the matter with George?' she asked.

Daphne's bewildered expression suggested that she hadn't a clue. Joan remained expressionless, having no wish to offer an explanation. When Melissa looked towards her, she merely shrugged her shoulders.

'I think it was something I said about Chester,' said Daphne, confirming that she did have a clue after all. 'I was praising him for coming up with the idea for a new series we're doing, when suddenly – Well, you saw what happened.'

'Oh, he's just jealous, that's all – jealous of Chester. You know what those two are like … always trying to outdo each other. It wasn't your fault, Daphne. Just a pair of silly little boys … or just one in this case.'

Melissa was so obviously sympathetic towards Daphne that anyone could see that they would soon agree again to share a flat. Joan could, so, nose in the air, she picked up her half-eaten sandwich and left without a word.

To return to her lonely reception desk.

Chapter 24

Planning Various Things

The Ugly Duckling was one. *The Emperor's New Clothes* was another. *The Nightingale* a third. Melissa had been busy. She'd found her book of fairy tales – a collection of Hans Christian Andersen's – and had spent the evening reading through it, selecting her favourites for the new series.

'I've thought of some clues as well,' she proudly told Mr Fothergill, who could hardly believe how industrious she had been and how enthusiastic she was. 'For *The Emperor's New Clothes*, we could have a coat hanger with no clothes on it hanging from a wardrobe. For *The Nightingale*, we could have a row of birds perched on the branch of a tree, with one of them having a key in its back to show it's a mechanical one. And for *The Ugly Duckling*, we could have one of those red herrings you like. But I'm not very good at red herrings, so I thought you'd better think of one.'

Mr Fothergill regarded that as a compliment, which pleased him no end.

'I shall give it some consideration,' he affirmed as modestly as he could. 'We'll be starting the series with *Little Red Riding Hood* – I wouldn't want to disappoint Mr Grounds – so we'll have plenty of time to come up with something suitable. And we'll do *The Emperor's New Clothes* second – I like that story. I must confess I'm not familiar with *The Nightingale*. But these are marvellous, Miss Morgan. Well done. You're not just a pretty face, it seems,' he said, smiling broadly.

Melissa didn't blush. But everything she did with her face suggested she knew she should have done. It was a long time since she'd last blushed at being called pretty. All she could do now was go through the motions.

Apart, that is, from telling Daphne at lunchtime what she'd done. Daphne thought she was doing a bit of boasting, and didn't like her for it. If there was one thing that really annoyed Daphne, it was when someone blew his own trumpet – or, in this case, *her* own trumpet ... which was likely to mean curtains for their intention to share a flat, if Melissa ever did it again. Chester, on the other hand, complimented her on her 'research', using what was an impressive-sounding word in order to ingratiate himself into her good books, with his usual purpose in mind. George and Joan, who had got into the habit of sitting together, agreed that all the tales had been done in jigsaws before and that Mr Fothergill should have carried on with the murder series, whatever the police said.

Inspector Fullerton didn't know what to say at the moment. The inquiries he'd instigated at the shops selling jigsaws had garnered no information regarding murderous-looking people. He was lounging back in his chair, gazing up at Detective Sergeant Carter who was standing on the other side of his desk.

'The thing is, Carter,' he muttered, as much to himself as to his assistant, 'the murderer almost certainly would have bought the jigsaws in the same shop; so if it was the same assistant each time who had served him, he would surely remember him.'

'Not necessarily, sir. He may genuinely –'

'Carter, don't interrupt me with what's obvious when I'm using my imagination. If the same assistant served him, it's possible that that he could remember him. How's that? Does that satisfy your pedantic mind?'

'I was only trying –'

'So … what if the assistant serving him was a different one each time? Would it prove worth while to go back to some shops, get all the assistants together and ask if they can recall any of the people who had purchased the jigsaws and whether there was any physical similarity between them – indeed, whether they were the same person? What do you think?'

'Could be a waste of time, sir. I'm not sure I'd like to –'

'Carter – I know I asked you a question, but you didn't really need to answer it. You could have kept your mouth shut and been a bit more helpful.' He got to his feet. 'No, by God, Carter, we're not going to sit back doing nothing. We are going to check those shops. We'll check those where the jigsaws have sold in the greatest numbers, and get all the assistants together and ask them exactly what I've suggested. Let's have another look at that list.'

*

Gregory was in his studio, lounging back in a tatty old armchair, pondering with disquiet his current situation. He'd been commissioned to do another painting for Fothergill Puzzles, and he wasn't happy about it. *Little Red Riding Hood* – what kind of subject was that for a serious artist? They'd ask him to paint *Goldilocks and the Three Bears* next ... or *Jack and Jill* ... or *Three Blind Mice*. It was humiliating. And he was expected to do it in such a way that no one would be sure what the painting depicted. How could he do that? Once he put in a red cloak and hood, everyone would know. And if he didn't put them in, how could anyone know it was *Little Red Riding Hood*? He smiled sourly. He could put in a *blue* cloak and hood as a red herring. Mr Fothergill would like that. Ha-ha! A *red* herring! A blue cloak and hood as a red herring instead of a red cloak and hood as a blue ... His smile disappeared. Maybe he should tell ol' Fothergill no. Just refuse to have anything to do with this new series. Tell him to get another artist – one who was used to painting silly fairy tales.

He looked across at his easel. It shouldn't be tainted, he thought, with stuff like that. He *was* a serious artist, damn it! And just to prove it, he decided, he'd have a drink or two before he got started.

Mr Fothergill had kept Mrs Fothergill up to date with the plans for the company's new series.

'We can't expect it to be as popular as the murder series, but I see no reason why it shouldn't appeal to our younger customers.'

'If they're still interested in stories about little Red Riding Hood,' Mrs Fothergill cautioned. 'These days I think they'd be more for jigsaws about Harry Potter and those toys in the *Toy Story* films.'

'Yes, I agree; but we don't have the rights to do jigsaws about those. And don't forget that until they do the jigsaws, they won't know it's about little Red Riding Hood. For all they know, it could be about Harry Potter.'

'Yes, but if there is a jigsaw on the market about Harry Potter, and they know it's about Harry Potter, they'll buy that one instead of ours.'

'I can't do anything about that,' said Mr Fothergill. 'We're always faced with competition, whether it's Harry Potter or … Buzz whatever his name is. And I'm not sure there is one anyway – not of Harry Potter. Not that I'm aware of.'

Mrs Fothergill got up from her chair. They had just finished dinner.

'Better wash up,' she said.

Mr Fothergill rose as well. 'I'll give you a hand.' He didn't like doing dishes, but he did like talking about jigsaws and he hadn't finished yet. He picked up a tea towel to do the drying. 'I must say, you know, I do admire that woman for standing up for what she believed.'

'Which woman?'

'Ms King.'

'Oh, her? Silly woman.'

'Well, yes. Silly but … she felt our jigsaws were doing – or could be doing damage to the nation's children and –'

'A very silly woman. Why – in this *Little Red Riding Hood* jigsaw you're planning to do, doesn't the wolf eat little Red Riding Hood's granny? What could be more violent than that?'

'That's what Chester said, I think…. Or was it George? Anyway, you're right, of course. It is violent – very violent. And yes, she is silly, but was standing up for what she believed, and that can only be admired.'

'She's silly. I can't admire what's silly.'

'Yes, she's silly, I agree. All I'm saying is that I admire her for standing up and being silly.' He chuckled.

Mrs Fothergill grinned. 'Or is it that you think she's pretty and you want to stick up for her?'

Mr Fothergill smiled. 'How could I think she's pretty? Don't forget I have Miss Morgan for a secretary. Who could be prettier than her? Apart from you, of course, when you were younger.' He put his arm around her waist and gave it a squeeze.

Mrs Fothergill blushed. She hadn't got as used to being called pretty as Melissa, so she still blushed whenever *anyone* called her pretty. Not many people did these days. In fact, no one did apart from Mr Fothergill. And even he had said 'when you were younger'.

She couldn't forgive him for that.

Gregory had had more than one or two drinks. He'd had six or seven, and as he swayed towards the drawing board on which he made his initial sketches, he couldn't positively remember what he was supposed to do. Goldilocks, wasn't it? Goldilocks or little Red Riding Hood. Both names came to mind. One or the other. Did it matter? Did he have a choice? He laughed tipsily. A red herring – that was it. One or the other was a red herring. Goldilocks – she was the red herring because little Red Riding Hood was red, not blue. So ... he had to paint Goldilocks in red as a red herring, with red hair ... No, she had to have goldy locks instead of red because little Red Riding Hood had red hair. That's why she was a red herring ... because whoever did the jigsaw would never guess she was supposed to be little Red Riding Hood.... Now we're getting somewhere, he thought.

He reached the drawing board, sat down on the chair in front of it, then leaned forward and down so that his head was slumped over the board. He felt depressed. Goldilocks ... was that what he'd come to – painting pictures of her, even if it wasn't really her? ... What a joke! ... What a big fat joke! ... Two fat jokes and a puzzle.

Edgar Rice Root wouldn't have thought it a joke. If he'd bought a jigsaw showing a picture of Goldilocks when he had to guess it was little Red Riding Hood, and later found out it was little Red Riding

Hood even though it was a picture of Goldilocks, and that Gregory Dawes was the man and artist responsible, he would have added the name of Gregory Dawes to that of Andrew Fothergill as someone to be chopped up with the axe he was now putting in his briefcase. He had already packed his suitcase with the clothes he needed for the six days' stay he had booked at the Mansard Hotel in London. That was close to where Fothergill Puzzles was based. Six days should suffice, he reasoned.

He was driving down there the following morning.

Chapter 25

Further Investigations

It was a Sunday. Cold, bright, rather windy, with snow forecast down south. Edgar would have set out in a hurricane. He had a mission – a mission to kill – and nothing the weather could hurl his way would thwart him. He was in a good mood. He switched the radio on and listened to some music as he drove down the motorway, keeping just below the speed limit; he wasn't one to attract the attention of police at any time – not if he could help it.

He made steady progress and didn't stop for a break at a service station till below Birmingham. There he had a chicken-and-salad sandwich with mayonnaise, a slice of carrot cake and a cup of tea. He would have his main meal later, once he had settled in his hotel and studied the lay of the land round the Fothergill Puzzles building. He wouldn't have time that evening to enjoy the city's sights or go to see a show. He could leave things like that till later in the week. It wouldn't do to make too hasty a departure after the murder.

Yes, it was a Sunday, but these days shops and stores opened on Sundays. And that was reason enough for Inspector Fullerton to send his men round, perhaps for the second time, to those that sold jigsaws. He concentrated on the bigger shops and stores. They were the ones likely to have more than one assistant to do the selling, and he ordered his men to find out as much as they could from any assistant who was present, but also to get the addresses of those who weren't and call round to speak to them to see if any information they could give matched anything they, the detectives, already had or would later obtain. He himself went to shops in Preston, Chorley and Leyland. It seemed pointless going as far south as Manchester, since the murders had occurred within a circle of which Preston was just about the centre. Fullerton had concluded that the murderer lived in that vicinity, including the coastal towns of course ... like Blackpool. It happened to be Carter who made the trip to Blackpool.

He had two calls to make there. All he got for his trouble at the first was a look of bemused disbelief from a manager who couldn't understand why the police were making inquiries about jigsaws; it was the first time he'd been approached about the matter. He should have been questioned before, and Carter could only imagine that certain of his colleagues weren't doing their jobs as well as he was doing his; but he kept to the original policy of refusing to explain why. Fullerton feared that if word got round about the unusual nature of their inquiries, the murderer might realise that the police were closing in on him, so he'd insisted that all his detectives say nothing about the murders and that if anyone asked why they were investigating jigsaws, they should hint at plagiarism of another company's products. Carter couldn't bring himself to do that, and felt all the more independent from Fullerton for saying nothing.

At his second call, he spoke to a young man with neat, highlighted hair who had spoken to the police before, and who – wonder of wonders – had something to tell Carter. Yes, he did recall a man with a wide fleshy jaw and narrow eyes buying a jigsaw of the sort described. It was his manner he recalled as much as anything – almost as if the man was slightly ashamed at buying such a thing. That was months ago, he said, and he didn't know who the man was or where he lived or came from – but he had seen him once in the shop since; that was why he remembered him now.

'Is that the only jigsaw he's bought?' Carter asked.

'As far as I know. But I'm not the only one who could have sold him one. Jessie could have done. Moira could have done.'

Hmm, thought Carter. Now was the chance to put Fullerton's plan into operation. He looked forward to doing so. Fullerton would be pleased if he knew he'd gone to such lengths to further the investigation. So shortly after, having obtained the addresses of both assistants from the manager, he was motoring to Marton, at the rear of Blackpool, to speak to Jessie, who, the manager assured him, would be of more help than Moira, who wouldn't remember her own name unless someone kept reminding her of it.

The house was a semi-detached house with a creaky wooden gate and a well-tended front garden. And wonder of wonders again, Jessie was in. She was a middle-aged, bespectacled woman with an old-fashioned perm in her gingerish hair, and if she'd ever been pretty it was a personal endowment she'd lost gradually over the period of time in which she'd borne three children.

As might be expected, her mouth dropped open when Carter introduced himself, confirming that she immediately assumed one of her children had been up to no good. But when Carter explained about the jigsaws, she invited him inside, offered him a cup of tea, which he accepted (as if to confirm his growing independence from Fullerton), and told him to make himself comfortable in the armchair by the window while she made it.

It was so warm and snug in the room that he'd almost dropped off by the time she returned. She brought him a biscuit too, which he nibbled while asking his questions.

Oh yes, she remembered such a man very clearly! Her immediate response took Carter by surprise.

'I'll tell you why,' she said. 'When he came to the counter to make the purchase, I told him I'd just bought the same jigsaw for my youngest boy. He already had the first two and I thought I'd get him the third for Christmas. Anyway, when I told this man he just smiled in a ... sickly sort of way. It was as though he couldn't care less. I didn't like him. But I remember him very well; I've seen him in the shop before.'

Hmmm, not a nice man, deduced Carter. Of course, it didn't mean that just because he wasn't a nice man he must be a murderer. It didn't work like that. Still, Fullerton would be pleased when he heard about him. Before he left, he wrote down as full a description of the man as he could from the woman's recollection of him.

On the other hand, he thought as he drove away afterwards, it would probably be a waste of time trying to find the man. Two assistants had sold a jigsaw to the same man … well, so what? Wasn't that just a coincidence? Fullerton was always going on about the difference between clues and coincidences. He'd look pretty silly if he told him about this man and all Fullerton did was pour scorn on him for not realising that it was just a coincidence.

So should he bother to tell him? Carter wondered about that all the way back to Preston.

Once Edgar had booked in at his hotel he wasted no time in walking the short distance to the Fothergill Puzzles building with the aim of finding a convenient parking place from which to watch the early-morning arrivals of the Fothergill staff – most particularly of Mr Fothergill himself. He wanted to know what kind of car he would be driving, so that later he could follow him and find out where he lived. He had already checked in the phone book and found three Fothergills who might be the person of interest to him. And one in particular was a strong favourite, living as he did only a mile or so from the company's base. But he had to be sure. He couldn't very well turn up at the wrong house and –

No; that wouldn't do at all.

As he casually strolled by the building, which was completely shrouded in darkness, he gazed across at it. Four storeys high and unremarkable architecturally, its front was made up of alternate rows of windows and pale-blue panelling. One look was enough; he didn't bother with a second. He found what he wanted in a side street almost opposite the entrance to the car park. If he could sit there in his car for a while as the workers arrived in the morning and watch out for Fothergill – whom he was sure he would recognise from the television – he could return in the afternoon in time for his departure.

With that settled, he went off to find a restaurant.

He wasn't one for eating Indian food, but a curry was what he had that evening. He wasn't sure whether he liked it or not; but he certainly disliked the waiter's constantly smiling face. It took all his powers of self-restraint not to tell him so – or to tell the woman at a nearby table to lower her voice, because she was getting on his nerves. It wasn't the time to cause a scene.

He went to bed early, rose early and drove round to the side street in good time for the workers' arrival. Fortunately, there was a space available. He manoeuvred his car into place and, spy-like, began to wait.

Carter wasn't the only detective to report that someone had been seen by different assistants to buy more than one of the jigsaws. There were four in all – and three of those were women ... which to any good cop meant that Carter's man was the most likely suspect, if he could be called that by any stretch of the imagination. Fullerton himself was told the name of a woman who had bought three of the jigsaws. Carter didn't have a name, but even Fullerton couldn't blame him for that. If the assistants didn't know the man's name, he could hardly expect Carter to provide it.

'It might be as well, Carter,' proposed Fullerton, 'if we got one of our artists to visit this Jessie and have him draw a picture of the man, so we have as accurate a likeness as possible. I don't suppose she'd mind.'

'I doubt it, sir; she seems a very cooperative person. Very nice too. She gave me a cup of tea and a biscuit.'

Up until then things had been running smoothly between the two detectives. Fullerton hadn't made a single snide comment about Carter's work in Blackpool. Mention of the biscuit changed all that. He stared at him

'She gave you a cup of tea and a biscuit? Would that be a chocolate biscuit, Carter?'

'No, sir.'

'A ginger biscuit?'

'No, sir.' Carter was turning red.

'Do you know, Carter, in all the time I've been a detective – nay, in all the time I've been a policeman, I've never been offered a cup of tea or a biscuit by anyone.... Did it have any cream on, your biscuit?'

'No, sir; it was just an ordinary ... shortbread, if I'm not mistaken.'

'Shortbread? Why, that's almost disappointing, isn't it? Didn't you complain and say you wouldn't settle for anything less than a cream or chocolate biscuit?'

'That would have sounded ungrateful.'

'It would, Carter, but sometimes one has to stand up for oneself or one would never get a cream or chocolate biscuit. And you haven't even brought me one, have you ... even if it was only a shortbread?'

'I didn't know you liked them, sir.' Carter was trying his best, but of course he was wasting his time.

Fullerton got up from his chair. 'It must be your winning smile, Carter.'

Amazingly, Carter wasn't sure whether Fullerton actually believed he had a winning smile.

Things were going to plan for Edgar. He had been in place that morning for the arrival of Fothergill's staff and he caught sight of Mr Fothergill in his car – a maroon Vauxhall. Nothing fancy, Edgar noted. Obviously a very boring man. Well, he'd have to be, making jigsaws for a living, thought Edgar. Such mental abuse of his imminent victim was understandable from his point of view. It safeguarded against any intrusion of sympathy. That wasn't likely to occur these days, but subconsciously he must have felt it was best to make sure.

Having seen the car, he devoted the rest of the morning to a visit to HMS Sheffield, in case anyone at his hotel later asked how he'd spent the day. But he made sure he was back in place an hour before the expected clocking-off time for Fothergill's staff.

It was still dark when the maroon Vauxhall eased out into the road. Edgar had to peer intently through the narrow slits of his eyes to be sure it was Mr Fothergill in the driver's seat; but it was and he set off in pursuit.

Traffic was heavy, which made for slow progress. Edgar was two vehicles behind the Vauxhall and that was ideal for his purpose. He feared losing him at traffic lights and having to go through the same procedure the following day; but as long as he kept on his tail, that was unlikely – though in fact it almost happened, when Edgar had to ignore a red light to stay in touch. If he'd been pulled up by the police then, it could have spelt disaster for his plans. He wasn't and before long he saw the Vauxhall turn into a road of rather large, semi-detached houses and then into a driveway. By then Edgar was right behind and could very easily have pulled up alongside and paid Mr Fothergill a visit there and then. But he drove past. He didn't want to park his car anywhere near the house; it wasn't how he worked. This day was all about surveillance. He spent the evening, first eating at a restaurant, then slipping back to where Fothergill lived and keeping a watch for ten minutes, then going to a nearby pub and having a drink, then returning to where Fothergill lived and keeping watch for another ten minutes from a different vantage point, then driving away before returning once more at around eleven o'clock to see when the Fothergills went to bed, which, conveniently for him (because by now he was getting cold and bored, they did almost immediately). At least, their lights went off, so they seemed to have done.

Then he returned to his hotel and went to bed himself.

By mid-afternoon the following day Fullerton had an artist's impression of the man described by Jessie and her colleague. It was a reasonable caricature of Edgar but hardly a photo-like resemblance of him. Fullerton peered down at it.

'I have a good feeling about this,' he told Carter. 'A gut feeling. Never ignore gut feelings, Carter. Just make sure they aren't stomach pains and you won't go far wrong. Of course, a gut feeling felt by an experienced detective isn't as reliable as that felt by an *in*experienced one. It seems to work subconsciously, if you ask me. All the years one spends investigating crimes seem to take root in one's mind, which then works psychosomatically on one's inner being, so that a good detective senses when he's on to something. And I tell you, Carter, this man' – he jabbed the portrait with his forefinger – 'is a genuine suspect. We need to find him, if only to eliminate him from our inquiries. First off, we'll have to check our photographic records to see if he's already in them. There can't be many people with as wide a jaw as he's got. Let's get busy.'

Chapter 26

Visits to Two Houses

Poring over the station's collection of photographs, Fullerton found someone whose face resembled that in the artist's drawing almost straight away. He jabbed his finger at the photograph, something he'd taken a liking to doing.

'If that's not him, it's his double,' he asserted confidently.

More like his double, thought Carter, who nevertheless wasn't about to argue and, on the basis of what he'd thought, would have been on shaky ground if he had.

'Come on, Carter. No time to lose.'

That was a ridiculous thing to say even if they *hadn't* any time to lose. Best to leave things like that unsaid in case they had all the time in the world. Nothing to lose, in other words, by not saying it. They could still hurry as much as they liked, but Fullerton wouldn't have risked making a fool of himself.

In any case, it took them only ten minutes to get to where they were going. It was a terraced house only a mile from the station – and not in Blackpool.

The man who answered the door to Fullerton's knocking had a wide fleshy jaw and narrow slits for eyes, but he wasn't Edgar Rice Root. He was Tommy Andrews, thief and benefit fraudster, but not a murderer – which might have explained his indignation on realising who his callers were, had he been asked questions about the murders. But he wasn't. He was asked if he'd bought any jigsaws recently.

'Who is it, Tommy?' came a cry from inside the house.

'The police,' shouted Tommy, turning to look back. Fullerton and Carter were still standing outside, and Tommy had no intention of inviting them in. A woman appeared behind him. She wore a thin, red-and-green striped dress which hung shapelessly down from her shoulders, and she had shoulder-length black hair, which was wet and uncombed. suggesting that she might have been drying it before curiosity got the better of her.

'What've you done, Tommy?' she demanded.

'I haven't done anything? What makes you think that?' he demanded back, momentarily forgetting the detectives' existence.

'You must have done something,' the woman insisted.

'Oh yeah – bought some jigsaws,' he scoffed.

'What – you've been buying jigsaws?'

'Have I heck as like! These geezers are asking me if I have.' He turned back to Fullerton. 'No, I haven't. What do I want with bloody jigsaws?"

Fullerton was perceptive enough to know that this was not the man they sought. Thieves lie all the time. Benefit fraudsters lie all the time. But this was one time when the thief and benefit fraudster was not lying; Fullerton would have staked his reputation on it. Carter obviously wouldn't have, because now he intervened.

'You mean you've never been to Blackpool to buy any jigsaws?' he asked, as if he deemed it a question cunning enough to catch him out. All it did, however, was give Fullerton a chance to save face.

'No, Carter – didn't you hear the gentleman say he hadn't bought any jigsaws recently. It's only if he'd bought any recently that we would be interested in where he'd bought them. Whether he bought any a long time ago and bought those in Blackpool is irrelevant to our inquiries. My apologies, sir. I hope you manage to convince your good lady that you haven't done anything wrong apart from buying jigsaws; I wouldn't want to cause disharmony in your household.' Saying which with a sarcastic edge to his voice, he turned on his heels and strode back to his car, followed by Carter.

'*Have* you done anything wrong, Tommy?' the woman could be heard saying just before Tommy slammed the door shut.

And then behind the closed door: 'Have you been buying jigsaws for another woman?"

Edgar spent the morning and afternoon doing things he wouldn't normally have wanted to do, like visiting the National Gallery and going to see the Houses of Parliament. He had to pass the time somehow before evening, and engaging in everyday tourist activities was the obvious way to do it. But every now and then he stopped to ponder how best to proceed once darkness fell. And occasionally his face broke out into a smile, for there was, he thought, a humorous side to his murderous plan. If everything went as expected, he would enjoy himself as he never had before.

His anticipation of doing so probably helped him to enjoy the steak he had beforehand. It seemed particularly tender and tasty, and the vegetables were well done too. A less conscientious person might have put the murder off for another day, preferring to stay where he was and indulge himself further with a bottle of wine. Not Edgar. He only had to think of red herrings and he was impatient to get the job done.

Yet he knew in his heart of hearts that this could be his last. The guy Fothergill would know who he was, and if he didn't finish him off – and his wife, if she was with him – his name would be given to the police and arrest would follow, if they could catch him, which, truth to tell, was more than likely, unless …

Best not to think about that.

The time had come. He paid his bill and left the restaurant. When he reached his car, he went to the boot, opened it, took out his briefcase, which he'd put there for safe-keeping, and was soon heading towards the Fothergill home.

There wasn't so much traffic on this journey and it wasn't long before he arrived at the road where the house was situated. He turned into it, scrutinising the Fothergills' house closely as he passed it. A ground-floor light illumined the room behind a pair of gold-coloured curtains. He must be in ... available, thought Edgar with a slight but evil smile.

He parked round the corner where it was most dark, then picked up his briefcase, climbed out of the car, shut the door quietly and then started walking back towards the house. He didn't hurry. He was on the alert for other people, for anyone who might be heading towards him and who then might be able to identify him later. Had anyone seen him, he would have crossed over as though heading away from the Fothergill home. But it was very cold and dark – not the kind of night when people ventured out unless they had to – and nobody else was about.

He reached the house. Other murderers might have become nervous at this point, fearful of unexpected circumstances, like visitors being in the house. Not Edgar. He walked up to the front door almost brazenly and rang the bell. There was a small light above the door, so he kept his face towards the house lest anyone should suddenly pass and look towards him. No one did. But a light came on in the hallway, a latch was turned and the door opened, revealing the enquiring features of Mr Fothergill. He wasn't used to getting callers at this time of the evening.

Edgar smiled broadly. Jessie was right: it was a sickly smile. Mr Fothergill perhaps wasn't so perceptive, for he returned it with a more welcoming one.

'Mr Fothergill?' Edgar began. 'I'm so sorry to trouble you at this time of night, but you know me from the letters I've sent you … Edgar Root.'

The name didn't immediately click.

'From Blackpool…. Remember?'

'Oh, yes – Mr Root.' As it dawned on Mr Fothergill who his caller was, it also brought a look of puzzlement to his face. What on earth was Mr Root from Blackpool doing here at his house?

'I just had to call round while I was in the area. I wanted to ask you to do me a favour.'

Mr Fothergill's expression became one of bewilderment. How on earth had he got his address?

'I'd like you to sign a copy of a book I have.'

'Oh? A book? What book would that be?'

Edgar tapped his briefcase. 'It's in here.' He made no move to bring it out, waiting for Mr Fothergill to invite him inside. 'It's an important one for your jigsaws. I think you'll find it interesting.'

Mr Fothergill was getting cold standing on the doorstep, and so was the hallway.

'You'd better step inside, then,' he said, without quite understanding what his visitor could want with his signature on a book.

'I hope I'm not disturbing you,' said Edgar. 'It is a bit presumptuous of me.'

'Not at all,' said Mr Fothergill as he led the way into the living room. Mrs Fothergill looked up from her chair to see who their visitor was. 'This is Mr Root, Vera. He's the gentleman from Blackpool who's written to me a few times. I've mentioned him to you.'

Mrs Fothergill's face expressed both surprise and concern. She immediately detected Edgar's sickly smile and she didn't like it. 'He wants me to sign a book. A most unusual request, Mr Root, if I may say so.'

'You may, Mr Fothergill. You may indeed.' Still standing, he unfastened his briefcase and reached inside, pulling out a large hardback copy of –

'This book … *War and Peace* by Leo Tolstoy…. You know it, of course.'

'Indeed, yes. I can't say I've read it. But we used it – Ah! I see what you're getting at. You want me to sign it because we used it in one of our jigsaws.'

'You did use it, yes – as a red herring. You caught me out there, Mr Fothergill. A very cunning ploy.'

Mr Fothergill, beaming, was reaching out for the book. 'Yes, I'll sign it. Happy to do so.'

Mrs Fothergill hadn't been won over so easily. She was studying Edgar very closely. What a strange man!

Edgar handed the book to Mr Fothergill, then reached inside his pocket for a pen, which he also gave him.

'If you would, write: "To a man I duped", then sign your name.' The smile was still on his face.

Mr Fothergill smiled as well, but now uncomfortably. That didn't sound very nice – duping someone. Still, it was probably meant in fun. He started writing.

Once he finished, he handed the book back to Edgar, who shoved it into his briefcase and then brought out something else.

A square piece of cardboard.

'Do you mind if I put this here for a second?' he asked, placing it on the settee.

Mr Fothergill gazed at the drawing on the cardboard. 'What's that?' he asked.

'Don't you recognise it, Mr Fothergill? It's a sign that appears in one of your jigsaws.'

'Oh, yes – a pawnbroker's sign. That's in … what? … our fourth jigsaw.'

'That's right, Mr Fothergill. Well done. You obviously know your jigsaws inside out.'

This remark didn't go down well with either Mr or Mrs Fothergill. It sounded sarcastic.

'And this.' Edgar reached into his briefcase again and extracted something else: a calendar. ''Do you mind if I put this next to the pawnbroker's sign?' He did so whether they minded or not. 'That's my red herring,' he boasted. 'You see the date circled there? Well, it isn't the date of a full moon. The police probably won't notice; they never seem to notice my calendars. But it's there – a red herring. You put one in your jigsaw and I've put one here.'

Mr Fothergill had come to realise that there was more to this visit than his Mr Root's desire to have him sign a book. He was shaking his head.

'Mr Root – what is this all about? I don't understand –'

Edgar had raised a forefinger in the air to silence him.

'And now this.' Once again he reached into his briefcase. 'The most important object of all.' When he brought out the axe, the mouths of both Mr and Mrs Fothergill dropped open, confirming that, although they still didn't know for certain, they both had a terrible fear that this man was about to become violent.

Certainty was achieved within seconds as Edgar, raising the axe above his head, lunged towards Mr Fothergill with every intention of bringing it down on his head.

As elderly and overweight as Mr Fothergill was, needs must, and he instinctively protected himself with both hands, seizing hold of Edgar's hands and by so doing causing him to lose his grip on the axe, which fell to the floor.

Mrs Fothergill was no less tardy in her reaction. She jumped out of her chair and flung herself on Edgar's back, causing him to lose his balance and follow the axe to the floor.

'Run, Vera!' cried Mr Fothergill. 'Out of the house!' She didn't need to be told twice. She raced out of the living room, followed by Mr Fothergill, and the two of them were out of the house in a trice, screaming and yelling.

'AXE MURDERER! AXE MURDERER!' cried Mrs Fothergill.

'AXE MURDERER!' cried Mr Fothergill, joining in even though it seemed a strange thing to be shouting.

Neither stopped running. They hurried across the road, still crying out at the tops of their voices. And to their relief doors started opening and figures emerged from other houses. They looked back towards their own house. Edgar hadn't come out as far as they could see. But now they were being surrounded by their neighbours. They were safe.

Chapter 27

But How Safe?

Edgar had gone. The police searched the house thoroughly before the Fothergills were allowed back inside, and Inspector Grainger assured them that they wouldn't be left alone for the rest of the night. Naturally, he plied them with questions about the man who had attacked them, and wanted to know the significance of the pawnbroker's sign and the calendar, both of which had been left on the settee. Mr Fothergill explained about the sign in the *Two Puzzles and One Murder No. 4* jigsaw, but hadn't a clue about the calendar, except that Mr Root, he recalled, had called it a red herring.

'He said something about full moons. I've no idea what he meant by that. There's nothing in our jigsaws relating to full moons.

Oh, but there is something you should know, Inspector. A policeman – an inspector like you – phoned me from Preston, I think it was …'

He told him about Fullerton and having to postpone his *No. 5* jigsaw because a murderer had been copying –

At which point Mr Fothergill fell silent, realising who Mr Root must be. He looked across at Mrs Fothergill, who was trying to compose herself in an armchair.

'It must be him,' he announced to everyone.

The astute Inspector Grainger didn't need to be told: he had already deduced as much.

'He called from Preston, you say?' he asked.

'Inspector Fullerton? That's his name, isn't it, Vera? Yes – Preston.'

There were more questions and more of the best answers Mr Fothergill could provide, and Grainger soon had a full picture of what had been going on. He wasted no time in contacting Fullerton, explaining what had happened and passing on the name of Edgar Root for him to investigate. He was even able to give him Edgar's address from the letters Mr Fothergill had received.

A policeman was left on guard at the house – actually inside the house, since it was far too cold to make him stay outside. The Fothergills were more than happy for him to be there.

'He can stay for a week,' Mr Fothergill quipped, to show he had returned to some degree of equanimity.

'He might have to,' replied Grainger. 'We can't leave you alone for a while – not till we find out where this man is.'

Edgar wasn't sure himself where he was at that moment. Having slipped out of the house and returned to his car, he had driven away without bothering too much where he was going. He knew he was finished now. The police would release his name to the press and television and warn people to be on the lookout for him, stressing how dangerous he was. There was no point in heading back to the hotel; all he'd left there was a change of clothes. He was going to get caught before long. Very quickly, in fact. His car would be identified somehow and the police would be watching out for that. His bank account –

Edgar realised it might be best if he took out as much as he could before his account was blocked. How long it would take the police to do that he didn't know; but ... but did it matter? Here he was driving round aimlessly to no purpose except to escape. And what was the point of that, if merely to delay the inevitable? He had to put it to use – to good use. Like killing that man Fothergill. He could still do it. At the Fothergill Puzzles building. And destroy the building at the same time, by setting fire to it. That would stop production of those damned jigsaws – his way of going out in a blaze of glory. A blaze of glory – ha-ha! Yes, that was what he'd do.

And now there was a point to driving round. He was looking for a garage where he could buy some paraffin. It took some time. The first garage he tried didn't sell it, but the man on duty told him where he could get some even at that late hour, and twenty minutes later he had two cans of it.

He then had to find his way to the building, and that wasn't easy. But eventually he turned his car into the same side street in which he'd parked earlier, and pulled up in virtually the same spot.

Then he sat behind the steering wheel for fifteen minutes, festering. He couldn't stay there all night. A policeman might pass at any moment, either on foot or in a car and catch sight of him. He had to act now ... either set fire to the building or break into it and wait there till morning and Fothergill turned up. If he turned up. That wasn't certain. The police might warn him against doing so … or they might come with him and search the building to make sure his attacker wasn't lying in wait. Still, it had to be one or the other – a break-in or arson for starters. It was the only way he could expect to get near Fothergill before the police found him. They were bound to have his car number by now; they wouldn't have wasted any time getting that. At least it was dark in the street; the car *was* in shadow.

Damn! He suddenly realised he could have done with a different coat to put on. Fothergill would have described the clothes he was wearing, so even walking about would be hazardous.

It would be best, he thought, if he could get in the building, hide somewhere till morning, and hope that Fothergill turned up without the police. But it didn't really matter one way or the other. He had his cans of paraffin. He could start the fire and use his axe on Fothergill in the ensuing panic. He hadn't forgotten the axe when he left the Fothergill house; he had it in his briefcase.

His mind made up, he opened the car door and climbed out. The cans of paraffin were in the boot. In a bag. Good thinking, that, to ask for one. He needed it to be able to carry both cans as well as his briefcase, which he needed to hide the axe. A few minutes later he was striding towards the Fothergill building, carrying all the required items.

Cleaners – they must use cleaners, he thought. But when? In the morning, before the other members of staff have arrived, or early evening, after they've left? And what about a security guard? Surely they'd have one. Yet the building was in darkness. That suggested no cleaners, but what about the guard? He could be in a small room in the basement, if there was a basement. Yes, there was bound to be. They'd need it to store all the things they used to make their jigsaws and boxes, like cardboard. So, if he could find a way of getting into the basement ...

He started strolling round the perimeter of the grounds, studying the building at ground level. There had to be an entrance somewhere, with steps leading down to a door or pair of doors. And there was – in the side of the building. There was space in front for a vehicle to pull up and be unloaded, so Edgar assumed he was right. The question now was: could he get inside without setting off an alarm? The stairwell was in complete darkness, so he would be able to work there without being seen, but ... was there a guard and would there be an alarm?

There'd be both, he knew. But he was past caring. If there was a guard, the axe would do just as well for him as it would for Fothergill. He walked on for a while, wondering what to do; but as soon as he could slip into the grounds he did so, and made his way quickly to the stairwell by the darkest route.

There were eight steps leading down to twin doors. Once at the bottom, he could hardly make himself out. He fished out his mobile phone and used the torch to study the doors. Could he prise them open with his axe? It was unlikely but he had to try. He took it out of his briefcase and pushed the blade as far as he could into the tight gap between the doors, working it back and forth to cause a larger gap as he tried to wrench one door away from the other. It was hopeless. He was frightened, too, of damaging the axe; he particularly wanted that in good working order for Fothergill. It would have to be a fire. That would set off an alarm, which would cause any guard inside to come running and, hopefully, give him the chance to slip inside the building while the guard was otherwise engaged.

Edgar unscrewed one of the cans of paraffin and emptied the contents on the ground, making sure that some of it ran under the doors. Then he climbed the steps, dousing each one with some of the paraffin from the second can. A piece of paper from his notebook, his cigarette lighter, a flame, the paper catching fire, the paper tossed onto the paraffin, and Edgar ran for cover behind a small brick building, which stood in a spot from where he could see whether anyone emerged from either the main entrance or the door in the side. If anyone did, he was bound to check around the building for other fires. That might give Edgar the chance he needed.

And it did. His plan worked a treat. The alarm sounded. Within a few minutes, having already extinguished whatever flames were spreading in the basement, a guard pushed open the doors and appeared in the stairwell, firing foam from the extinguisher on what little was left of the flames in the well. It had never been a big fire, but the guard would have had to call the fire brigade, so Edgar had to act swiftly. He did so when the guard, as hoped, went round the rear of the building to check that no other fires were burning.

It was just as well he didn't dawdle, for the guard was gone for no more than thirty seconds. By the time he got back, Edgar was down the well and hurrying through the basement to the stairs – stairs he would climb to the top floor, where he intended to hide till morning.

The fire brigade turned up quite quickly. The guard explained what had happened. The firemen did a quick check inside the basement but, based on what the guard had told them, saw no reason to explore further. They jokingly praised him for his ability with the extinguisher and urged him to join the brigade, then left the way they had come with a sense of anti-climax and disappointment.

The guard was duty bound to advise Mr Fothergill of such an incident, and when he did he told him that the fire was probably the work of youngsters with nothing better to do. Mr Fothergill thought differently. And when he, through the policeman staying at the house, informed Inspector Grainger, who had left a short time before, they agreed that the arsonist had to be Edgar Root.

'Trying to burn your building down,' Grainger declared. 'He's certainly got it in for you. I think I'd better go and speak to your security guard, and find out whether he noticed anyone resembling Root's description loitering about. It's probably him, but we shouldn't jump to conclusions, however ridiculous it seems in this case not to.'

'Yes, well, I'll be coming too, to see what damage has been done,' said Mr Fothergill.

'Not without one of our lads to accompany you,' insisted Grainger. 'In fact I'll pick you up myself; that'll be quickest. I should have stayed there.'

When they arrived, the guard Bob Pritchard – sixty years of age, grey-haired and deferential – showed them the two cans they'd found in the well, but said he hadn't seen anyone suspicious.

'Have you checked inside the building to make sure no one got in" Grainger asked.

'I had a quick look, yes,' claimed the guard, 'but I've no reason to think anyone did. I don't see how anyone could have done. You can see the damage to the doors is minimal; I was able to lock them again once the fire had been put out.'

He wasn't being entirely honest in saying that; but the last thing he wanted was to have to admit to being careless, especially after being the hero of the hour in the eyes of the firemen.

Grainger nodded, wanting to believe him. And his nodding must have persuaded both himself and Mr Fothergill, who was happy to accept the detective's greater experience in such matters. So before long, without conducting a search themselves inside the building, Grainger and Mr Fothergill left. Grainger did give instructions that any police in the area should keep it under surveillance and watch out for Edgar Rice Root, the man suspected of having started the fire; but oh dear, he could have done rather more himself.

If Inspector Grainger was lax here in pursuing his man, the same could not be said of Inspector Fullerton, who, on being given Root's name and address, set off for Blackpool without delay. He made it a big operation too, with Carter and other policemen following on. Even if Root was in London, he might not live alone and a thorough search of the premises would have to be made. He might well be the murderer they'd sought for years, and every little thing indicating his guilt would have to be gathered.

They had to break in, but that wasn't a problem. Finding evidence was. Edgar had been very careful in that respect. They did find the jigsaws.

'No time to do them now, Carter' quipped Fullerton, who was in a better mood than usual. 'Just keep searching.'

If Inspector Grainger had searched the Fothergill Puzzles building, he might have well have discovered Edgar in the canteen. That's where he was. Once he was sure that no one was coming to look for him, he made himself comfortable in a chair, ready to disappear into the toilets on hearing anyone. He would hide in a cubicle there, and if the worst came to the worst and someone pushed open the door to reveal him, he had his axe.

And indeed, Bob Pritchard made his rounds an hour later, when Edgar had to make himself scarce very quickly. But Bob didn't check the cubicles in the women's toilets and so was able to return to the security guard's den with his head intact.

He should have made a second inspection of all the floors a few hours later but didn't, so Edgar was left undisturbed for the rest of the night and spent some of the time sampling the canteen's cakes, as well making a cup of coffee to help him stay awake.

Chapter 28

Another Meeting

The Fothergills didn't sleep well that night, despite the presence of Constable Craig downstairs. Mrs Fothergill took a pill eventually but Mr Fothergill refused to do so; he thought it best to be 'ready for anything', and that wouldn't be the case if he was half-doped on drugs ... which hardly helped to set Mrs Fothergill's mind at ease, so she ended up taking another one.

Very early in the morning, Constable Craig was replaced by Constable Marks, and an artist arrived to draw a picture of Edgar according to the Fothergills' description of him. Grainger had hoped that a photograph would be obtained from Root's house and faxed to him, but none had been found. Mr Fothergill asked the artist to draw a picture for him as well, so he could show it to the staff at Fothergill Puzzles.

'I have to go in to advise them of what's happened,' he explained. 'I can't leave them in the dark, especially after the fire at the building. Who's the say that any one of them might not be attacked?'

Constable Marks informed Grainger by phone of Mr Fothergill's intention in that respect, and handed the phone to Mr Fothergill for the inspector to pass on some advice.

'Keep your eyes open and your car locked until you arrive. And even then make sure he's nowhere about before you get out.'

Unnecessary advice but well meant.

As was Mrs Fothergill's when she told him to 'Be careful'.

Well, he was always a careful driver, so that came naturally; but yes, he showed a greater degree of care on his way to Fothergill Puzzles in everything he did and everywhere he looked. It was what some might call 'living on the edge'.

And he followed Grainger's advice on coming to halt in the car park, as close as he could to the entrance to the building. He looked all around, then climbed out and scurried across to the glass doors. He found Joan at her desk, putting things in order as though she too had just arrived. Her worried expression told him she already knew about the fire. Mr Fothergill wished her good morning as usual, but this time without the friendly smile that always accompanied it.

'I'll need to see you and everyone else in ten minutes. Please come up to my office then, will you.' He didn't stop to answer any questions she might want to ask but headed for the lift, momentarily fearing that when the lift door opened, Edgar Rice Root would leap out with his axe. But it didn't happen, and Mr Fothergill was safely hoisted to the second floor.

Melissa was already there at her secretary's desk.

'Have you heard about the fire?' she asked without first greeting him.

'I have, Miss Morgan. I had to come last night when it was reported. But something else has happened which you all need to know about. Would you please bring everyone to my office. And I mean everyone'

Melissa loved meetings. She liked going round to everyone and passing on what was really an order. It wasn't that it made her feel important as Mr Fothergill's emissary: it was more a case of having a get-together with her colleagues and almost having a bit of fun, bearing in mind how comical Chester could be, as he no doubt would be about the fire. He'd think of something to make them laugh. So she hurried off to do as Mr Fothergill had requested.

While he was waiting, Mr Fothergill rehearsed what he would say. He rather liked the idea of relating the dramatic events of the previous evening. How their mouths would drop open, confirming their astonishment! An axe murderer in his very own home – it was hard to believe in the cold light of day. If they didn't believe him, he … Well, of course they'd believe him. The fire – who did they think had started that? It may be that not everyone had heard about the fire. He had the picture of Edgar in his briefcase. He brought it out and studied it for a few moments. Yes, it was like him. He placed it on his table, face down, so they wouldn't notice till he dramatically turned it over and declared: 'This is the man'.

He walked to the window and gazed out, his arms clasped behind his back. A police car was in the car park. Inspector Grainger had probably ordered one there to make sure that everything was all right. One couldn't be too sure, of course, but there was no reason to think it wasn't. Mr Fothergill was more worried about being at home without a constable on guard. That could be nerve-racking, especially for Vera. But how long could one expect the police to act as their very own security squad? The sooner that man was behind bars, the better – for everyone, if he was that murderer they were trying to catch.

The members of his staff started to arrive, including Doreen from the canteen; Melissa hadn't forgotten her – though without checking in the ladies' toilets for anyone else. Mr Millar had brought the few members of his production team as well.

'Come in, please,' Mr Fothergill welcomed them, and waved them closer. 'Gather round, so you can all hear what I have to say. Is everyone present?'

'Where's the fire?' demanded Chester.

That was what Melissa had been waiting for. He meant it as a joke, meaning what was all the fuss about, though in fact there had been a fire. Melissa thought it was funny and laughed. She was the only one – though Daphne smiled, more in sympathy with her than at Chester, whose jokes, frankly, were beginning to bore her; she did, after all, share an office with Chester when he wasn't touring the country and she heard a lot of them.

'Well, actually, Mr Grounds,' replied Mr Fothergill, 'as you may know but some may not, there has been a fire – one started deliberately – by the side of the building in the stairwell to the basement. And when I tell you of what else has been happening you'll understand that it was unlikely to be the work of mischievous youngsters.'

Suddenly everyone became more interested. They looked at each other inquisitively, then focused their attention on Mr Fothergill again.

'Last night,' he began, 'Mrs Fothergill and I were attacked in our own home by a man wielding an axe.' The listeners' mouths dropped open, confirming their astonishment, as Mr Fothergill had predicted. They also looked at each other again to confirm that other people were as astonished as they were. 'Fortunately we were able to escape before he caused any injury to either of us. Mrs Fothergill was obviously very upset by the incident – as, I must confess, I was – and is still trying to come to terms with it. Understandably. For that reason I shan't be staying here too long today; I want to return home to help her get over it.'

'Quite right,' murmured George, causing heads to nod in agreement.

'As for the man, he may well be a murderer …' – a gasp from Melissa triggered a smaller one from Daphne – 'a serial killer, in fact'

There were gasps all round now. 'You must be joking,' said Chester, giving expression to a cliché that other people, having thought it, had resisted uttering.

'Indeed not,' said Mr Fothergill. 'I wish I were. There's no doubt he's the murderer sought by that inspector who stopped us producing our successful *Two Puzzles and One Murder* series … because he was apparently copying the pictures in our jigsaws by leaving the same clues at the scene of any murder he committed.'

'Is that why he tried to kill you – because we stopped making jigsaws he could use for his murders?' wondered Chester. Melissa didn't know whether this was a joke or a sensible question, so she didn't laugh, even though she felt like doing.

'No, that wasn't it. Strange as it may sound – and it is strange – I got the impression that he didn't like being fooled – 'duped' was the word he used – by our red herring in *No. 4*. I suppose it made it harder for him to work out which murder was being depicted and he didn't like it.'

'So that's why he – presumably it was him – started the fire,' deduced George. 'He resented the company so much he wanted to burn it to the ground… That's ridiculous.'

Nods all round, and in some case with open mouths again, confirming unnecessarily what their nods were making clear.

'Yes, we're pretty sure it was he who started the fire,' said Mr Fothergill. 'But he didn't succeed in burning the building to the ground. That's good but there's also a bad side to it. If he hasn't done it yet, he probably still wants to do it, just as he may still want – will obviously still want – to murder me. And perhaps some of you as well.' Mr Fothergill paused here to let his last words sink in.

Mouths were getting tired but they still dropped open, including Alysse's for the first time.

'For that reason,' Mr Fothergill went on, 'you must be on your guard at all times, till this man has been apprehended. When that will be, of course, is impossible to say.' He picked up the drawn picture of Edgar and held up for everyone to see. 'This is the man.'

At which point the door swung open with a crash, revealing a figure with an axe in his hand.

Edgar Rice Root had come for Mr Fothergill.

He hadn't expected to intrude on a meeting, and no one present had expected him to do so. Their mouths were still open, so they didn't have to drop them again. They simply stared at him. Goggled at him – till Mr Fothergill, whose eyes weren't very good at a distance, finally identified the man standing there and, pointing at him, cried out:

'That's him! That's Root!'

Edgar must have known there was no getting away. He could have started wielding his axe at everyone, but with so many people there he might have killed only one before they pounced on him. He realised that in the instant he made up his mind to go for the man he most wanted: Fothergill. He raised the axe above his head and lunged forward without the animal cry one might have expected, but with hate-filled eyes and gritted teeth.

Bravery is often an instinctive thing, before thought brings out the coward in all of us. As Edgar rushed by, it was Chester who acted first, instinctively reaching up to grab the arm in which Edgar was holding the axe. He clung on desperately as Edgar tried to shake himself free. George acted almost as quickly, seizing Edgar's other arm, so he couldn't wrestle Chester away. And Melissa – bless her! – wasn't about to let anyone use an axe on the best employer in the world, so she bent down and grabbed one of Edgar's legs, picking it off the ground so he couldn't get any purchase from it. Naturally, that persuaded Daphne to do the same with the other leg. With both legs off the ground, Edgar fell back and soon had five or six people on top of him. Try as he might to use the axe on one of them, he couldn't, and was soon disarmed.

'Keep hold of him!' Mr Fothergill urged excitedly. 'Don't let him up. Keep him on the ground. He's a dangerous man.'

As if anyone needed telling!

In due course Edgar was formally arrested and taken away by the police. Mr Fothergill rang his wife to tell her the good news, and gave everyone the rest of the day off to help them recover from what must have been for some, he assumed, a traumatic experience, bearing in mind that when they arrived for work, they must have been expecting a very ordinary and perhaps tedious day. It would hardly be right to want them to carry on with their everyday duties. Even so, it was close to lunchtime before anyone made to leave; they preferred to spend the morning discussing what had happened and finding out from the internet about the murders in Lancashire during the previous few years.

It was Melissa who brought a fitting climax to the day's events with a brainwave she had.

'We should make a jigsaw of it,' she suggested as a joke.

But Mr Fothergill decided otherwise. It wasn't a joke. It was a very good idea. A jigsaw of how the people employed at Fothergill Puzzles had brought the career of a serial murderer to an end. A jigsaw of how Mr Grounds had grabbed his arm as he plunged towards his prey; of how Mr Miller with an 'e' had seized his other arm; of how Miss Morgan and Miss Muir … had wrapped their own arms around his legs and brought him to ground, and how then other members of the staff had dropped on him before he could wriggle free. Such courage deserved its celebration – and would have it in the form of a jigsaw.

Everyone was in favour. Of course they were.

Mr Fothergill was already thinking of a follow-up and a future series.

'Do you know what we'll call it?' he said. '*Two Puzzles and One Attempted Murder.*' He looked round for approval.

Chester slightly amended that. 'Or *Two Puzzles and One Attempted Real-life Murder.*'

'Yes,' agreed Mr Fothergill. 'It was most definitely in real life. I can vouch for that. I think we all can.'

So the jigsaw's production was set in motion. Gregory was phoned and asked to supply a painting of what had happened when the staff at Fothergill's performed heroics to save the life of their employer; Mr Fothergill went into great detail about that. Not having been present at the incident, Gregory thought he must have been drinking to hear what he was hearing. Either that or Mr Fothergill himself had taken to drink. But no, he found out later that everything Mr Fothergill had said was true, and so he started his painting.

It took him an awful long time. The trouble was Melissa. Try as he might, he couldn't paint a face as pretty as hers. He destroyed one painting after another before he was satisfied. And then he settled for a moderate likeness only because he'd had a few too many drinks again. He would have been satisfied then if he'd painted her looking as plain as Joan … who for some reason, I'm afraid, he forgot to include in the picture.

Nor did Joan's fortunes improve. She never got to share a flat with Melissa or Daphne. And taking to booze herself in her lonely abode, she was often legless in a very different way from how Edgar had been that day in Mr Fothergill's office.

On the other hand, Melissa and Daphne didn't get to share a flat either. When Gregory presented his picture at the next meeting, everyone agreed that, as he'd painted them, Daphne looked prettier than Melissa. That started an almighty row between the two which to this day has not been forgotten.

So both of them are still living at home with their mothers.

Printed in Dunstable, United Kingdom